Azad Younesi was born in Baneh city, Kurdistan province, Iran. He received a master's degree in safety, health and environment from Tehran University. In 2021, due to political problems, he became a refugee in Britain, and now he lives in Glasgow.

azad135862@gmail.Com

Dedicated to freedom-fighters of Rojava, who made great sacrifices for liberty and independence of their land.

Azad Younesi

MERCILESS

AUSTIN MACAULEY PUBLISHERS™

LONDON • CAMBRIDGE • NEW YORK • SHARJAH

Copyright © Azad Younesi 2024

The right of Azad Younesi to be identified as author of this work has been asserted by the author in accordance with sections 77 and 78 of the Copyright, Designs and Patents Act 1988.

All rights reserved. No part of this publication may be reproduced, stored in a retrieval system, or transmitted in any form or by any means, electronic, mechanical, photocopying, recording, or otherwise, without the prior permission of the publishers.

Any person who commits any unauthorised act in relation to this publication may be liable to criminal prosecution and civil claims for damages.

This is a work of fiction. Names, characters, businesses, places, events, locales, and incidents are either the products of the author's imagination or used in a fictitious manner. Any resemblance to actual persons, living or dead, or actual events is purely coincidental.

A CIP catalogue record for this title is available from the British Library.

ISBN 9781035837991 (Paperback)
ISBN 9781035838004 (ePub e-book)

www.austinmacauley.com

First Published 2024
Austin Macauley Publishers Ltd®
1 Canada Square
Canary Wharf
London
E14 5AA

1

A few years ago, the day after the big breast Sabir disappeared, a tall man got out of his car.

"Stay in the car. I will come back soon," he told his family, who were sitting in the car. He entered the mosque in the village. In the toilet he washed his face and hand and brushed the dust off his pants. It was noon, a little before midday prayer; he came out of the mosque and went to a small store across to the mosque. A muscular man with Kurdish head scarf sat inside.

"Hello, Haji[1], How are you? Give me a pack of Winston cigarette, a red one please," He said to the shopkeeper.

"Hi, I am not Haji but a chief of this village. You said the red one?" the shopkeeper asked.

"Yes, red one please."

Chief Salim, besides doing his chief job, had a small store. He put some frippery and a few stuff in the store; his store had one refrigerator for water and other drinks. Chief gave him one pack of the red type cigarette.

---

[1] Islamic term, a person, who has visited Mecca is called Haji

Araaz took some torn money out of his pocket and gave it to him. He dragged one cigarette out of the pack. "Sorry, chief, is there any house for rent in your village?" Araaz asked.

Chief took a look at his dress and said, "Based on your accent, you must not be from here, am I right? Are you alone, or …?"

"I am from the outskirts of Krmashan[1], living with my wife, son and my mother," Araaz replied.

Chief welcomed him. He remembered that Rozhan and Sabir had a house for rent. Araaz was staring at the stowed roof and burnt parts of the store.

"What is your job?" Chief asked.

I do some business inside the city. I carry cargo. Renting a house inside the city is too expensive. Besides, they wouldn't rent house to strangers. It should be cheaper in the suburbs.

The chief looked at Araaz's untied shoelaces.

"I will be thankful if you find a house for me."

"Excuse me, what's your name please?"

"Araaz, sir."

"Yes, Mr. Araaz, a few months ago, Mr. Sabir and his wife told me that, the downstairs of their house is available for rent, but I don't know …," Again, he stared at Araaz's untied shoelaces and Araaz noticed the gaze of Chief's eyes

---

[1] Kurdish city of Iran

on his shoes, while he was playing with his cigarette. He put his cigarette between his lips, bent down and tied his shoes.

"Have you got their numbers?" Araaz asked.

The chief again looked at Araaz's shoes. Araaz lit his cigarette, bent down again and this time, put on his shoes completely.

"It's time for mid-day prayer. After the prayer, we will go to Sabir's house together," Chief Salim said this and stood up to close his shop.

"Wait, sir! The children are hungry. They haven't eaten anything since morning. Let me take something for them." Chief took three bottles of water, two cakes and one biscuit for them.

"Let them have these so that they won't be hungry until we go to my house for lunch," Chief said.

"No thanks, we don't want to bother you," Araaz answered.

The chief didn't take money from them.

"You are not disturbing but are guests and guest is God's beloved ..."

He closed his shop and set off with Araaz. Some people gathered around his car.

Easy, he didn't get hurt, he will forget soon.

Araaz quickly went to see what was going on. His son, Dlir, was crying in his mother's arms, and the area around his eyes were slightly red.

"What's wrong, dear Dlir?" Araaz shouted.

9

"Nothing. The inside of the car was very hot and the sunlight was directly on our eyes. We came out under this walnut tree, but a dry branch fell and struck Dlir's head. God bless these people, they helped a lot," his mother answered, breathing hard. She took a bottle of water and drank a little. "Where have you been, kid? You left us here for two hours."

His wife took Dlir from him angrily. Chief greeted them. "He was with me," Chief answered. "Mr. Araaz, that building down there has a special water creek for women. Take your family there, then bring Dlir to the mosque to see the fish in the pond."

Araaz accompanied them to that building, then he hugged Dlir and went after chief Salim towards the mosque.

"Haji Basit won't come today, that's why no one said Azan," the chief grumbled slightly. Chief Salim wasn't so tall. Although he was over seventy years old, but he looked fifty. He was put on a Kurdish Moradkani[1] suits and a black hat and heads scarf on his head.

"Oh, Haji, what do you want from this mosque? Why don't you leave us alone?" Chief continued grumbling.

His grumbling was because of the struggle between Haji Basit and Imam of the mosque. Half of the village stood with Imam and the other was with Haji Basit. The struggle between them was so complicated that one day in the mosque yard, a big fight happened between them. A stone hit Haji Basit's head and he passed out. His head was injured and he was taken to the hospital. The day after this fight, he entered the

[1] a special style of Kurdish suits

village with a bandaged head accompanied by his fans. They brought so many cars and sacrificed two sheep to welcome him, but the police didn't allow anyone to enter the mosque. Inevitably, they went to Haji Basit's house. On their way, the fans of Imam made fun of Haji Basit's bandage. They said, "The stone was a blessing for Haji. He has achieved the sign of bravery."

Chief Salim and some elders of the village went to the police office. They, along with the police officer who was also looking for a solution came to this conclusion that each day, only one of them would come to the mosque and say the call (Azan) to prayer, and same for the Friday prayer. The elders went to Haji Basit's house and informed him about the decision. At first, Haji Basit was very angry …

"I will never accept it. For God's sake, they wounded me in the house of God," Haji said.

Amidst the noise and threats of Haji's fans, Chief looked at his companions and said, "Thanks God, it ended well. You and Imam Abeed made a big mess. That's why we came to you to inform you about our decision. You have to accept this. If not, you both must go out of the village. Your dispute is old, we all know about that, and it is not related to our village."

Haji Basit touched his head and looked at the chief and police officer and said, "Ok …okay, I accept only because of your attempts."

Imam Abeed also accepted the new rule and peace returned to the village again.

It was Haji Basit's turn and he hadn't come yet. The poor student of the mosque was waiting to say the Azan.

"If he doesn't come …Mr. Araaz, will you come for praying?" asked Chief.

"Next time. My clothes are not clean and appropriate today," Araaz answered.

"Ok, wait here, I will come back soon."

Araaz took Dlir to the mosque pool. It was full of small and big fish; Dlir had just calmed down. He crushed his biscuit and threw it into the pool, the fishes gathered around it quickly. Araaz washed Dlir's face, while he was waiting for Chief to finish his prayer.

"That is not true, maybe one day Haji Basit couldn't come, neither could Imam another day."

"That is not true, that no one say Azan."

Two people came out of the mosque with Chief.

They were talking about the dispute between Haji Basit and Imam.

"Let it be like this for a while, we will see what happens. Let's go, Mr. Araaz," Chief said.

Araaz's mum came out of the spring and got into the car, but his wife was waiting for him under the shadow of the walnut tree.

They got in the car and went towards Chief Salim's house.

"We don't want to disturb you; it is not a good time," Araaz said.

"You are not disturbing at all," assured Chief Salim.

Dlir was sleeping in his mother's arms. Chief's house was below the castle of the village. A narrow path surrounded by some large blue stones that glistened in the noon sunlight. The car could hardly pass through it. They got off the car.

"Here, this is the house."

Araaz looked at the village and its surroundings. The blue sky had a piece of dirty cloud left over from the farewell of spring. Some new, big houses were seen among the old and dilapidated houses. The green colour of the plain had turned yellow. Chief's wife was in the yard looking for the broken parts of flower pot. She welcomed them and went into living room – a big room with a well-arranged wooden ceiling that had a pillar in the middle. Some pictures of Qazi Mohammed[1] and Mala Mostafa Barzani[2] were hung on the wall. Another picture of a fourteen to fifteen-year-old young man who had just grown a moustache was hung in a blue frame in front of other pictures next to the Ayatul Kursi[3] board. There was a small picture of Dr. Qasemlu[4] below the picture of Leader

---

[1] Kurdish great leader and founder of Mahabad Republic in 1946, he was hanged by the Pahlavi dynasty in 1947.

[2] Kurdish great leader and general of the Mahabad Republic. He was start

Ailul uprising in Bashur (southern part of Kurdistan)

[3] Islamic term, a surah of Quran

[4] Kurdish politician and leader. He was born in 1930 in Wrmi (a Kurdish city in the west of Iran). After the Fall of Qazi Mohammad, he continued to his study in politics in Tehran and Prague. After graduation as a Ph. D. he started teaching in the School of Economics in Prague. In 1979, after the Islamic revolution of Iran, and started his civil activities. Because of the conservative ideology of Islamic regime, that blocked all the road of peaceful negotiation, he started the armed fight against the invasion of Iran on Kurdistan. In 1989 Dr. Qasemlu, on the table of negotiation, got assassinated by some agent, related to Islamic regime, in Vienna.

Qazi Mohammed. Araaz looked at the pictures before he sat down.

"My father was Leader's peshmarga[1]."

The chief took the photo album from the shelf and sat down.

"Mr. Araaz and his family have just arrived and they want to stay here in our village," Chief informed his wife.

"You are very welcome!" Chief's wife greeted them.

She brought Dlir a pillow and a blanket. Chief Salim took a deep breath and started to show Araaz the pictures. In one of the pictures, his father and two other armed men were behind Qazi Mohammed, next to the Red Bridge of Mahabad[2]. His father was a tall man with a big moustache. Araaz realised that the picture inside the blue frame was his son. Chief got up and opened the window, a gentle wind brought the scent of basil and plants from the garden into the house.

"You're very welcome again." Chief repeated.

"Thanks a lot."

Chief and his wife lived alone. Their eldest son worked in the agriculture department in Sna[3] and their other son was killed in Saddam's aerial bombardment during the Iran-Iraq war. His daughter had recently married one of his nephews. Chief set the table. Fariba went to the kitchen to help Chief's

---

[1] Kurdistan soldier is called Peshmerga, especially in south and east of Kurdistan.

[2] A city of Rozhhalat and the bith place of Qazi Muhammad

[3] A city of Rozhhalat, Sna (Snadezh)

wife. Daya Halaw, Araaz's mum, was preparing tobacco for her cigarettes. Araaz winked at her.

She got the point and realised Araaz's gesture.

"Ok, ok! I won't smoke. I am just prepare them," said Daya Halaw defensively.

"Thank you for the lunch. May God bless you!" Araaz said.

"Hope you enjoyed, sorry for any inconvenience."

Araaz took the tea tray from Fariba and brought it for Chief. They drank the tea together and then they went towards Rozhan's house. Rozhan's house was not so far away. It was a really hot day.

Chief pointed to some houses on the other side of the river, "That two-storey house with a blue door is Rozhan's house."

At that time of the year, the river didn't have much water and was more like a small stream, hence there was no need for a big bridge on it. Chief looked at the river again and said, "It hasn't rained well this year, we are in the middle of August, but the fields are thirsty and dried."

The song of a bunch of ducks made Dlir laugh.

"Now the river is like a stream, but in spring and autumn, you will see its wrath."

A few months later, Araaz remembered these words of Chief when the flood took his mother away.

"Stop the car on your right hand under the Van tree."

Araaz stopped the car under the big Van tree. Chief got out of the car before them, went to the house and knocked on the door. No one answered. He knocked again.

"Hello?"

Araaz lit a cigarette and went to the back of the nearby abandoned house. That house looked like a ruin. The only sign of life was the Mulberry tree with its branches over the yard wall.

He had a cigarette on his lips. When he unzipped his pants to urinate, his eyes suddenly fell on a dagger stuck on the wall's crack and blood was dripping from it. It had a colourful wooden handle. He wanted to take out the dagger with fear, but whatever he did, he could not take it out. On getting Fariba's calls, he zipped up his pants and took a deep breath of his cigarette, and while looking at the bloody dagger, he took Fariba's hand and together with Fariba left the place.

Chief threw a small stone towards the upper floor window and shouted, "Open the door, Mrs. Sabir!"

The curtains were flowing and the window was opened. The rustle of Rozhan's slippers announced her arrival.

She was wearing a green Snay dress, with small red flower on its theme. She had a red scarf that covered her whole head which was tied at the back. She opened the door.

"Oh, sorry! It is you, Chief Salim. I was asleep."

She greeted him quietly while she was looking at Araaz's family secretly.

Chief said, "Sweetie, you and Mr. Sabir told me that your downstairs portion is available for rent. Mr. Araaz and his family are from Krmashan. They couldn't find a house inside the city, that's why they came here. They are nice family if—"

Rozhan didn't let Chief finish his speech,

"Sabir has not been home since yesterday, and no one knows about him."

From the redness of her eyes, it was clear that she had cried a lot. She was holding herself by leaning on the door.

"Sabir packed some stuff and went off. His phone is switched off, his father is also unaware of this," Rozhan said, her eyes were full of tears.

"Easy, my girl. He has been annoyed much recently. He will come back, I am sure," Chief assured her.

Rozhan was a short woman with a flat face; a few strands of her blonde hair were visible under her hood. She had cried so much that her eyes could hardly be seen. Her two big breasts aroused every man's desire.

"I don't know, Chief, it is up to you," said Rozhan.

"Don't worry, we also agreed on the rent price."

Rozhan looked at Araaz and his wife and welcomed them.

"Come inside, please."

Chief went in first.

The house had two bedrooms, a hall way, a kitchen, bathroom and a toilet.

"We didn't have time this year, otherwise we would have painted it," said Rozhan.

Araaz and Fariba wandered in the rooms. Fariba especially looked at the bathroom and the kitchen.

"There is one stove there, Mr. Araaz, you can use it too," Rozhan said.

"Thank you so much, we don't have any stove."

Araaz turned on the stove to check it.

"Ok, Mr. Araaz, I have to go. If you need anything, let me know," Rozhan said.

Chief Salim came to the yard and stood near some leftover stuff, left after the house repair.

Daya Halaw, who had fallen asleep, woke up by Araaz's voice, and got out of the car. She took out some house-hold items from inside the car-trunk and brought them inside.

"Sorry, Chief, what happened to Sabir?" Araaz enquired.

Chief Salim bent down and wiped his pants and answered, "Sabir, son of Sir Ali, a village teacher, was a very shy and quiet guy. Rozhan's father didn't want his daughter to go to university. He wanted her to get married. As soon as Sir Ali asked for Rozhan's hand for his son, Sabir, he accepted with no hesitation. The wedding ceremony was held quickly and they forced Rozhan to marry Sabir, despite her wishes. Sir Ali quickly built this house for them."

Chief went towards the old house, near Rozhan's house and looked inside through the window that was broken by the village kids.

"There was no news from Rozhan and Sabir for a while. They didn't seem to have a problem. Sabir rarely left the house out. Sir Ali and Rozhan's dad went to see what happened. When they got there, they saw Rozhan sitting, sad and dejected.

"Sabir is sick," Rozhan told them. "His breasts have been growing recently and they are getting bigger, day by day."

Sir Ali and her dad took Sabir to another room and took off his clothes.

"Oh my God!" Sabir's dad got very upset. Sabir didn't listen their pleas to see a doctor. Rozhan's brother, who was mentally retarded, found about it and spread it among the village. One day, on his way to the mosque, Sabir was followed by the village kids.

'Sabir big breast! Sabir big breast,' they started chanting.

"Since that day, no one has seen him. Many people say that Sabir got affected by Rozhan, since she also has big breasts."

Araaz couldn't control himself and burst out of laughing.

"It is impossible, it is not her fault," Araaz responded.

"Another question, Chief. Whose old house is that?" Araaz asked.

Chief was about to open the car door, but with Araaz's question, he turned around and looked at the Mulberry tree, whose branches spread out of the yard, and took a deep breath.

"This house is as old as our village. I heard from our grandfather that years ago, during the rules of the colonel Venis Khan[1], in the autumn, the gypsies used to come around the village and set up tents. One of those gypsies named Rahman axa Ashpoka, built a house in this place on Khan's command. Rahman axa, who had travelled many countries, gave the map of the world, drawn on a deer skin, to Venis Khan and as a reward, Venis Khan allowed him to build this house. Nobody knows where and when Rahman axa died, but he has many children. Every few years, one of them shows up and lives here for a while, and then suddenly disappears."

Chief brought them two lamps.

"This is my gift for you, Mr. Araaz!"

"Thank you, Chief! We are disturbing you too much today."

They cleaned the rooms. Rozhan brought them two sheets and said it will help until you buy a curtain.

They hung the sheets on the window, Rozhan took Dlir upstairs and put him to sleep.

---

[1] Kurdish social rank, upper than a chief in a village

It was evening when Araaz came over and parked the car at the door.

"Bring it inside, Mr. Araaz, the yard is big," said Rozhan.

He had bought a lamp, Kettle, teapot and some other staff. Fariba took the things from him. There were four stairs to their floor and Rozhan's house was upstairs, facing the court yard. Their house had a wide window facing the yard.

"Mr. Araaz and Miss Fariba, please come to my house for dinner tonight," Rozhan invited them.

"We will not disturb you anymore; enough for today," Araaz said.

"Don't say that," Rozhan insisted and went inside.

"Stand up, Hama, we have guests," said Rozhan.

Her brother, Hama, stared at TV and watched cartoon.

"Hey, I am talking to you," Rozhan asked.

"Ok, who's the guest?" Hama asked.

After Sabir left the house, Rozhan's dad sent Hama to be her companion. Hama was about 20 years old. He was mentally retarded. His favourite activity was playing Drum, which he had learned from Darvishs[1].

"Sorry, Miss Rozhan, for disturbing you," Araaz said.

"Don't say that. I was alone, God sent you to me."

Dlir was sitting in his mother's arm, rubbing his face with tomato. There was a pacifier in his mouth. Although he was more than two years old, he was still being breast fed.

---

[1] Islamic term, one special approach of Islam, who doing some chanting by playing drum and another musical instrument

"Hello, Mr. Hama, how are you?" Araaz greeted him.

Hama, who was lying down, without looking back at him, took the

TV remote out of his mouth and asked him, "Where are you from?"

"The outskirts of Krmashan."

"The police officer is also from Krmashan."

He started laughing.

Daya Halaw quickly fell asleep! Araaz was lying down and looked at Dlir. Somehow, everyone was tired. Fariba came in and turned off the lamp. She had hung a small mirror on the wall. Her hair was always short, but Araaz liked it long. She combed her hair in front of the mirror. She was wearing long men's clothes. She felt someone hug her from behind.

"My soul." Araaz put his face on her hair and kissed the mole on her neck. Fariba was tall and fleshy, and her eyes were liked a deer. Araaz removed the glasses from her eyes and rubbed her breasts tightly.

"Shame on you! Your mother hasn't slept yet," Fariba whispered.

Suddenly, a fear like a thunder clutched her heart.

"Araaz! My brothers will find us!" Fariba uttered.

"Don't worry, my sweetie, nobody can find us here," Araaz assured her.

One by one, he unbuttoned her shirt. Araaz and Fariba were distant relatives, but they loved each other too much. Their first meeting was in university library. She was wearing a blue and white dress.

"I'd like to invite you to lunch." *Araaz invited me after some days.* Fariba described their first date with Rozhan.

It was really surprising because I always thought Araaz was in another relationship. I never thought one day he would propose to me.

"Hello, Mr. Araaz, what brought you here?" Fariba asked.

"I had some job here. Besides, I also wanted to see you," answered Araaz.

Fariba knew the reason well; it was clear from his eyes.

"I don't want to bother you, Mr. Araaz."

"No, I am free."

"Do you remember that night when you were invited to our house? I was well aware of you. Even for a moment, you didn't take your eyes off me.

The restaurant was near the university. They chatted until the evening.

"Sorry, it is too late; we want to close the shop." Shopkeeper interrupted their conversation.

The owner of the restaurant was shocked by all this talk. Araaz was staring at Fariba's necklace, which left its line on her white skin.

"I really wanted to kiss you," Araaz said.

But Fariba's family were against this marriage. "I won't let him even put my daughter's body on his shoulder," This was her mother's word.

They forced Fariba to marry someone else; everyone was happy about this.

"Thank God, the groom is university professor. He is rich and our daughter is also happy."

Araaz had parked the car near the groom's house. He lowered the window and lit a cigarette. He was waiting for the right moment. The alley was dark. On that cold night, the wind penetrated the heart of darkness ruthlessly, the street light bulb turned off and on frequently. Daya Halaw was sitting in the back seat with closed eyes, praying nonstop with her rosary. It was past mid-night. Araaz threw out his cigarette, closed the window and put his head on the steer. Daya Halaw was still praying.

Suddenly, the sound of the opening of a door broke the silence of alley. A woman came out running towards the car. Araaz got off the car and hugged her. It was Fariba.

"My darling, I can't live without you," she cried.

They got into the car and set off towards Hamadan quickly. They stayed in Hamadan for a while. Araaz worked as a taxi driver of his car. Dlir was born after a couple of months. Fariba's brothers found their address, that's why one night, Fariba and Araaz secretly packed some stuff and run away towards Bana city. They wished that life would show them it's nice face after all the darkness.

Araaz used to go to the city early in the mornings, and Fariba was busy with home holding and her son. Daya Halaw used to sit under the Van tree and knit yarn; her tobacco bags were her close friends. From time to time, she rolled a cigarette. Sometimes she mixed a little green grass from a smaller bag with her tobacco.

"God bless you, Araaz," she would say and prayed for him. After finishing her cigarettes, she would get up, throw away her cane and go to the edge of the river laughing, then come back again. She remembered her youth, the good old time, when she lived in Halabja[1]. Her husband was Democrat party's Peshmarga. All Rozhhalat [2] parties had their own office in Halabja at that era. Daya Halaw was a young beautiful girl. Her father, who had a toggery shop, was a Baghdad university student in sociology field. When the Barzani uprising began, because of some seminar, he got fired from university and was imprisoned for one year. In prison, he lost his left eye under the torture. After prison, he got married and opened a shop, but he never gave up on his ideology, and his connection with Rozhhalat parties were getting stronger. Once, Ahmed and his friends came to his shop, meanwhile Halaw brought lunch for her father. They saw each other. Ahmed, who was a handsome young guy, fell in love with Daya Halaw at first glimpse, and they got married quickly. On the wedding night, some people came out of nowhere and took her father away; no one saw him after that night. Some said that the security service took him and he was killed under torture, while others believed that he was sacrificed within the Bashur[3] parties' competitions. Ahmed was a manly and proud boy; he often did the secret mission of party inside the Rozhhalat. At the chemical bombing of Halabja, I was only able to save Araaz and then, accompanied with some fellow citizens who survived, we walked towards

---

[1] Known as Martyred Halabja, a city of Bashur (south Kurdistan) that has been massacred by the chemical bombardment of Saddam. Hussein, in 16 March 1988, during the Iran-Iraq war. More than five thousand have been killed.

[2] The east part of Great Kurdistan is called Rozhhalat.

[3] The southern part of great Kurdistan, that nowadays is semi-independent and has a regional government

the border of Iran. On our way towards Sarpelzahaw, trucks of Iranian army took the displaced women and children. We dwelled in a camp in Sarpelzahaw. With her cousin's help, Daya Halaw raised Araaz and secretly travelled to Halabja and searched all places for her husband several times, but nobody had any trace of him.

"He must have been captured in Islamic Republic prisons," people said.

That's why she looked Wrmi, Krmashan and Sna prisons for him. Unfortunately, there was no sign of Ahmed. When Araaz grew up, he visited the office of Democrat party in Koya, searching for his father. One of the officials told him not to look for him anymore. He said, "When Mr. Ahmed got informed about the chemical bombing in Halabja, he walked towards the office of party from Qandil[1] Mountains, but unfortunately, he lost the way because of heavy snowfall and he was lost to the mountains.

Daya Halaw had a bad knee pain. The doctors prescribed surgery for her, but she didn't accept, that's why Araaz mixed grass[2] with her Tobacco. It reduced her pain.

"God bless you, Araaz, you stopped my pain." As for the job, Araaz would bring TV and air conditioners home, hide them inside the car, then he took Fariba with himself to be safe to cross the police check points. Gasoline price got higher, that's why he changed the car fuel to CNG gas. He was leaving early in the mornings with Fariba, more often towards Tabriz and cities around, because it was safe.

---

[1] A mountain near the borders of Iraq, Iran and Turkey [2] A kind of maijuana

25

"People say this city has a very cold winter," Daya Halaw said while she was knitting her wool.

Araaz responded, "Mum, spring is not over yet, don't scare us."

"It is mountainous and snowy region," answered Daya Halaw.

Rozhan had been sick lately, she had a pain in her belly. Her mum brought Miss Zinat to treat her.

"It's nothing, just your bellybutton." The villagers all visited Miss Zinat when they got sick. Most of them like to be touched by Miss Zinat's rough hands. It was more like a nostalgia for them. That day, Rozhan also got better under Miss Zinat's hands.

"Here it is, your bellybutton had moved to the right side. You might have lifted some heavy things or you must have jumped the stairs," said Miss Zinat.

"Jump what? I am not a kid. I just helped my neighbour and carried some stuff for them."

Rozhan's mother interrupted them.

"Why did you help them?"

"Did you rent out your house? Where are they from?" Miss Zinat asked.

"They are from Krmashan. It has been around one week since they arrived here."

"Couldn't you find a better family than these gypsies?"

"They are a great family, why would you say that?"

Rozhan pulled her dress up to her navel.

"Honey! It is a bad habit that you don't fasten a bra! Give me that cup," Miss Zinat scolded Rozhan.

Miss Zinat put her hand on Rozhan's stomach, while she talked about Krmashan region.

"People say, Hasan Zirak[1] was poisoned at the time he worked in Krmashan radio station."

"What are you talking about? Hasan Zirak died by cancer a few years after working in Krmashan, and I wonder what this has to do with my tenants," Rozhan retorted.

Miss Zinat put the cup on her belly and pushed it hard.

"Don't move! How do you know? Maybe he got cancer because of that poison."

Rozhan took a look at Miss Zinat and as the pressure of the cup got stronger, she closed her eyes.

"It won't go back to its place in one treatment session. We need two more sessions: tomorrow and the day after. Oh, I almost forgot to ask, what about your husband, Sabir?"

This question messed Rozhan up and she looked at her mother.

Her mother answered, "What about him? Oh, Miss Zinat, we know nothing about him. What can I say? This is our bad fortune."

"Sabir was not a good match for her, we all knew that ...People say he has been seen in Sullymani[2], wearing Arabic dress." Miss Zinat finished her words by this and then left. Under the tree, she saw Daya Halaw.

"Hey Miss, are you the new tenant?"

Daya Halaw, after a harsh cough, looked at Miss Zinat and answered her greeting.

"You have to be from Krmashan," asked Miss Zinat.

---

[1] Kurdish most famous singer

[2] Kurdish city in Bashur of Kurdistan and north of Iraq

"Yes, how do you know? Come and sit please!"

"Although I have to go, but I will stay with you for a couple of minutes."

Daya Halaw stood up and greeted her.

"What was your name?"

"Zinat."

"I am Halaw."

"How come you came here?"

"My son, Araaz, had no job. Here, because of the border, there are better job opportunities. Inside the city, the rents were so expensive. Villages are cheaper, that's why we came here."

Miss Zinat took one cigarette out from her pack and looked for her lighter, but she couldn't find it.

"You are very welcome here, but this place is also like other places; the main job is Kolbari[1] that is not a safe and secure job, because our children either become frozen in the snowfall on the mountain, or be killed by the bullet of police."

"Have you got a lighter?"

Daya Halaw lit up the cigarette for her.

"Rozhan's mum told me that you have arrived. Poor Rozhan, she had bellybutton displacement," Mrs. Zinat inhaled her cigarette deeply, looking for something new to

---

[1] kind of job in Kurdistan, especially in Rozhhalat (east of kurdistan), that Kolbar carrying the cargos by himself and crossing the border. Kolbar is a person who carry the cargo. Kolbari is a hard and dangerous job, because the border between Iran and Iraq is mountainous region, but the bad economic situation imposed this kind of job to the people.

talk about, touched her forehead and said, "Rozhan never had a good chance in her life. Look at her husband."

"Where could her husband be?" Daya Halaw asked.

"I don't know. People say he has been seen near central mosque in Sullymani. They say he was wearing Arabic clothes, putting on a mask on his face so that no one could recognise him."

Daya Halaw brought the bag of tobacco and started rolling cigarettes. She mixed a little bit from the smaller bag with it.

"I didn't know that you also smoked, Daya Halaw," Mrs. Zinat said, astonished. "Smoke one from my pack, here you go."

"No thanks, I like tobacco more, and since Araaz brought me this green type, my pain has decreased, God bless you, Araaz."

"What pain?" Mrs. Zinat enquired.

"My knee, my back …"

"Maybe it is your bellybutton. Should I touch your belly?" Miss Zinat asked.

"I don't know. But this tobacco makes me feel much better."

She lit her cigarette, inhaled deeply and continued, "Araaz told me not to smoke more than one time in a day; it is dangerous. Besides, it is also so expensive."

"You are absolutely right. Let me see that."

"Here you go."

"Miss Zinat took the tobacco and smelled it.

"Oh, it smells awful, what is this? I wonder if we can make a herbal medicine from it."

She smashed some with her finger and sniffed it, then wiped her hand with her pants. A squirrel jumped up and down on the tree and occasionally glanced at them.

"Let me roll one cigarette for you, just try it," Daya Halaw suggested.

"You said it is expensive …" Zinat answered.

Daya Halaw rolled one cigarette for her.

"Don't put too much."

"Don't worry!"

Daya Halaw lit a cigarette for her and inhaled softly and said, "Not too bad."

Daya Halaw got high and stood up,

"Let me bring some water for you."

Miss Zinat didn't answer. She inhaled all the smoke deeply. After a minute, she started to laugh. She laughed so much, that her breath was about to stop. Then she stood up and turned around the tree and laughed. Daya Halaw brought back a bottle of water and two glasses.

"Oh my God! Miss Zinat, what happened to you?" Daya Halaw shouted.

"That squirrel attacked me two times. It had a plans to eat me." She giggled and laughed loudly.

"Easy, the same thing happened to me when I smoked for the first time."

Miss Zinat got high, she jumped and laughed historically, and without putting her shoes on, she crossed the river and left. Rozhan's mum stuck her head out of the window and said, "Mrs. Zinat has gone crazy!" and looked at Daya Halaw for a while and then got back inside to help Rozhan.

Daya Halaw drank a sip of water and went after Miss Zinat and called her a few times, but no use …

"Where is the tobacco bag?" she wondered.

She looked everywhere for it.

She wondered if Miss Zinat took it, then she answered herself, "No, she forgot her own shoes here."

She looked every place for the tobacco, but she couldn't find it. She turned back to the tree again, and looked up on the top of the tree.

"Oh, how could this evil take it away?"

Daya Halaw got confused. Suddenly, Hama (Rozhan's Brother) came out with his drum in his hand. He walked a few steps forwards, then he stopped and looked at his drum and played it for a moment, and then started to walk again. He faced Daya Halaw.

"Hello, Daya Halaw, may I play a bit for you?" Hama said.

He didn't wait for her answer and started to play.

"Hello, sweetie Hama," Daya Halaw said. "How are you?"

"Good, me good."

Daya Halaw looked at him and said, "Can you take that bag down for me, please?"

"Sure, I can," answered Hama, who was sure about his abilities most of the time.

He put his drum down and climbed the tree and as soon as he caught the bag, threw it down immediately. It hit Daya Halaw's right in her face.

"Oh, my eye! I am blind," Daya Halaw cried.

Hama was laughing and tried to catch the squirrel!

"Come down, Hama, it is dangerous," Daya Halaw shouted. Hama didn't care at all; he was busy catching the squirrel.

Suddenly, Hama cried, "Help me, help me! Rozhan, please help me!"

Rozhan and his mum came out.

What happen? Rozhan's mum asked.

"Help me!" Hama shouted again.

"I am sorry," Daya Halaw apologized. She was blushing.

"What happened, Daya Halaw? Why would you be sorry?"

"That squirrel took the tobacco bag up on the tree. I asked Hama to climb the tree and bring it down for me," Daya Halaw explained.

"What squirrel, Daya Halaw! It was Miss Zinat who threw it up. She had gone crazy," Rozhan's mum enlightened her. "Come down my little boy."

"I am afraid I can't," Hama answered.

At the time, Dlir came out without pants and started crying. When Hama saw Dlir in that situation, he burst out of laughing and forgot everything and his fear was gone. Hama came down the tree and ran towards Dlir and hugged him.

The next day, Miss Zinat came again to treat Rozhan's bellybutton.

"She is better now," said Zinat.

She put the cup on Rozhan's bellybutton. Rozhan's mum turned on the stove to make tea and said,

"Sorry Miss Zinat, we woke up late today. Last night we couldn't sleep because of a barking puppy."

"You are absolutely right. I just served morning in my house."

Rozhan remembered yesterday and she was smiling secretly. Her mum was also laughing, but Miss Zinat was smart and changed the topic and said,

"Your new tenants are great. Daya Halaw is so funny. Yesterday, we were so busy that I forgot my shoes."

The excessive talking and the pressure of Miss Zinat's hands made Rozhan angry.

"It is not finished yet?" Rozhan asked.

"Wait! Yesterday, I was afraid of something, but thank God this is not that," said Miss Zinat.

"I wonder if you are pregnant!"

Rozhan got angry by her words and said, "What did you say? It is impossible!"

"You are absolutely right, honey, this girl has no luck at all," said Zinat.

It was obvious that Miss Zinat had just taken a bath; her hair was still wet. She said good bye to them and took a sneak peek at the tree, looking for Daya Halaw. She went towards Daya Halaw quickly.

"Hello, dear."

Daya Halaw had just started knitting yarn. She wanted to knit a blouse for Fariba.

"Hi, how are you? Come sit beside me," Daya Halaw greeted her.

"I don't want to bother you, I just want to take my shoes," Miss Zinat said.

"Don't be shy, it happens to everyone."

Miss Zinat asked, "Where can I find this tobacco?"

"I don't know, only Araaz can find this."

"You are absolutely right, Daya Halaw. I want to tell you a secret. I have a cousin who has been sick for a long time. She is angry all the time, and always has disputes with her husband."

"It is easy, I'll roll a cigarette for her," offered Daya Halaw.

"You are so kind, God bless you."

Miss Zinat took her shoes, and then left. In the afternoon, she and two other women came back to Daya Halaw. They said hello to Daya Halaw.

"How are you? You're welcome, Miss Zinat," said Daya Halaw.

"Daya Halaw, this is my cousin that I told you about, and that one is my neighbour," Miss Zinat introduced them.

Daya Halaw took off the bag of tobacco and rolled a cigarette for them.

"This tobacco is very strong; you have to inhale a little and take it back quickly."

Miss Zinat took out her lighter and lit the cigarette and took a deep breath, then passed the cigarette to her cousin. They all did the same until it got back to Daya Halaw. They looked at each other and repeated this circle again. The cigarette was not finished yet when Miss Zinat went towards the river laughing. The other two women also ran, but towards different direction. They laughed historically and then left. From that day, the shadow of that tree and Daya Halaw, became the rebirth centre for dead laughter of the villagers' women. They would come and take two puffs from Daya Halaw's cigarettes, then leave happy and high. The laughter that never came to birth near their husbands and relatives. They brought many gifts for Daya Halaw. The gifts were different and included yogurt, milk, egg and even rosary and chewing gum …that's why when Araaz and Fariba returned in the night, they got surprised by all the stuff.

Fariba and Araaz took a look at each other. While they saw yogurt, milk, eggs and Dlir who come to them and called their names with two eggs in his hand. It came to a point that in the evenings, ten to twelve women, most of them above fifty years old, gathered around Daya Halaw under the tree. They chatted, laughed and spent a good time together. Sometimes, Hama joined them by his drum and played for them. Rozhan, who had Dlir in her arms, was watching them from the window.

During day time Dlir never separated from Rozhan, that's why he nagged at nights, when he came back to his parents. One day, Hama shouted loudly from distant,

"Hey, Haji Basit has been arrested."

Miss Zinat, who was looking at Hama, burst out laughing and grabbed the cigarette from Daya Halaw and inhaled it deeply. She didn't pay attention to Hama's word at all. Capture of Haji Basit was not important for them. Not only Haji Basit, but none of the men's capture was of any importance to them. Hama noticed that nobody really cared about his news. He looked at their red eyes and played for them in confusion.

2

Around evening, they stopped near the "cold fountain" and got out of the car. Araaz took a look at the back of his car to see the damage to it, because they had an accident in the afternoon.

"Is it serious?" Fariba asked.

Araaz didn't pay attention to Fariba at all. The trunk had been damaged seriously, and he was cursing repeatedly.

"This much hurry for what? Are you a booster, I don't know!"

He lit a cigarette and sat next to Fariba. Fariba took a small mirror out of her bag and looked at her face; a few strands of her hair had turned white, but her face was the same student girl's face, with the same sparkle in her eyes. She looked at Araaz like a crazy deer and said,

"Why don't you pay attention to me? I have been calling you for an hour!"

"When did you call me, sweetie?" enquired Araaz.

"Enough, for God's sake, I am not important to you."

Araaz held her hand, grabbed the mirror from her, and looked at the mirror and said,

"I am getting old, Fariba, Am I right?"

"Oldness is a sleeping guest of all human bodies, and it grows up like a baby; shows itself in the facial wrinkles and white hair."

Araaz held her hand tight and looked west.

"What about death?"

"Enough, Araaz, why do you talk about these things on this sad evening?"

"Let's go. I miss Dlir so much!"

They stopped in front of Chief Salim's shop. He wanted to check if chief knew someone who could repair their door.

The shop was crowded.

"Hello, Chief Salim," he greeted.

"Hi, Mr. Araaz, give me a moment, I'm coming."

After a while, Chief came out of his shop. He approached Araaz and said,

"Sorry, Mr. Araaz, a problem came up. Haji Basit and son of Said Zada had been arrested naked. Haji Basit claimed that he was sick and he came to him to pray for him. They had been taken to the police station. What's up? Are you okay?"

"Thanks, our door hinge is broken. Do you know a person to repair it?"

While they were talking, a young guy come to Chief and whispered something in his ear. Chief said to Araaz in hurry,

"No problem, I'll tell Haji Baxtyar to come and fix it for you."

"Thank you, Chief," Araaz said and then he left.

"What are you doing, Fariba?" Araaz asked.

"Nothing. This TV fell on my bag."

Araaz lifted the TV and Fariba picked up her bag.

"Oh, Araaz, my mirror is broken!"

"Easy, tomorrow, I'll buy a new one."

"I liked it too much, I had it since I was kid."

They arrived home, then they carried the TV inside together. Daya Halaw came forward and said, "Welcome bride and son."

Dlir was sleeping in Rozhan's arms.

"He has been sleeping for a while," Rozhan said.

"Thank you, dear Rozhan."

Rozhan put a blanket upon him and handed Dlir to Fariba.

"The door is not fully closed. Your mother is still awake," Fariba whispered.

"Not to worry, I heard her snoring."

"Is Marlon asleep?" asked Fariba.

"No, he is awake and ready," answered Araaz.

She put on her memorial necklace. Her necklace had some gold pieces, surrounded by orange stone in a circle shape. It was one hundred years old. Father of Daya Halaw had given this necklace to Daya Halaw as a gift, and Daya Halaw had also handed it down to Fariba.

"What about my Ashmol? Is she awake?" Araaz asked.

"Get off me, bad boy, don't touch me!" Fariba persisted. "Do you hear that sound? It is a dog barking outside."

"Leave it."

"The voice of a dog was getting closer, until it woke Dlir up."

"Not a good time, puppy," Araaz murmured. He put on his clothes and turned on the light. There was a white poppy at the door.

"Go away, doggie," shouted Araaz.

The puppy stared at Araaz and barked again.

"What happened, Araaz?" Fariba shouted.

"It is a small puppy."

"Bring it inside!"

"Ok, I'll bring it in."

Araaz lifted the dog and took it inside. Daya Halaw, who was woken up by all the noise, got confused when she saw Araaz with a puppy and said, "Oh my God! What is that puppy? Don't touch it. It is dirty!" she uttered.

"Why are you calling it dirty, mum. This poor puppy might be hungry."

Fariba's eye sparkled in happiness, and she touched the puppy's head kindly.

"Don't look at me like that," Araaz gestured at Fariba.

They poured some milk for it. It was not barking anymore, and it took a peek at Araaz and started to eat. Next day, they didn't go out and stayed home.

Like any other day, Daya Halaw took the carpet and went under the shadow of the Van tree. When she got there, she noticed that somebody had scratched the tree in several parts and put a Kojila[1] on it.

"How could somebody do this to you?" She was shocked.

A man with Kurdish head scarf came out from behind.

"Hello, Miss."

He had a stick in his hand.

"Hello, dear!"

"I was thinking, is it okay to attach some Kojilas on this tree, until we can make some bitter gum out of it. Every year

---

[1] The villagers in Kurdistan, make chewing gum from Van tree (Daraban tree). For this, they scratch some part of the tree and attach Kojila below the scratched part, until the liquid of the tree drops down and is collected inside the Kojilas. At the end, they collect the liquid to make gum from it.

at the end of summer, we do it. This gum is like a medicine, Miss."

"Isn't it too soon for that?" Daya Halaw asked.

"No, it is the right time; by the way, I am Haji Baxtyar, Chief Salim has sent me to fix your door."

"Oh! You are welcome. Come with me," said Daya Halaw.

Fariba got up quickly, put on her clothes and called Araaz to stand up!

Araaz opened his eyes once and went back to sleep again.

"Ok, I'll deal with you later," Fariba warned Araaz and went outside to greet Haji Baxtyar.

"Haji is here to fix the door," Daya Halaw informed Fariba.

"Ok, okay!"

Fariba looked at the puppy that was still sleeping, and she brought a bottle of water and went to wake Araaz up. She removed the blanket from his head and dripped the water on him. Araaz stood up like a soldier.

"Haji Baxtyar is here to fix the door."

"Who?"

"The carpenter, Haji Baxtyar."

"Okay, why didn't you say so earlier?"

Araaz put on his clothes and went to Haji Baxtyar.

"Welcome, dear Haji, come on in," Araaz greeted him.

"How are you? Which door is broken?"

"Here, this one."

Haji looked at the door, then took off the hinges.

"I cannot fix it today. Tomorrow, I'll bring my staff and complete the job."

Haji Baxtyar was not so tall. He had dyed his moustache black and from time to time, he touched his moustache.

"Ok, Haji, you're welcome."

Out of Araaz's house, Haji looked at the tree and Kojilas again. Daya Halaw was sitting under the tree. He took out a cigarette and lit it up.

"If it is possible, please take care of the Kojilas. It should not be touched by the children."

Haji Baxtyar requested Daya Halaw.

"Don't worry, I'll take care of them," Daya Halaw assured him.

Dlir was afraid of the puppy.

"Easy, Dlir, nothing to fear, it is also baby. Look how beautiful it is!"

Fariba lifted the puppy and took Dlir's hand and went in the yard. Araaz was sitting on the stairs.

"What should we call it?" Araaz asked.

"He has a name, Haji Baxtyar. What else should we call him?" Fariba answered.

"I am talking about the puppy."

"You want to keep it?"

"Yes, we do."

Dlir jumped up Araaz's arms.

"Tell me what should we call it?"

"I don't know, you say it!"

"I don't know …we call it Ashmol."

"Quiet, don't make fun of this."

"Don't worry, nobody knows the meaning of Ashmol."

"How about we call it Marlon!"

"Okay, we call it Marlon for male and Ashmol for female, it's settled."

Fariba blushed, but she accepted the deal. Araaz grabbed the puppy from Fariba, looked it over to find about its sexuality and suddenly burst out laughing, and then took it back to Fariba.

"Haha! Its name would be Ashmol! Take it," said Araaz.

"No!"

"You don't believe me; you can see yourself."

"But what if the the people asked about the meaning of it."

"Just answer them, they don't know what we really mean by Ashmol."

Rozhan had washed a pan of clothes, and she was coming out to spread them in front of the sun. She thought Araaz and Fariba were out of the house, that's why she didn't wear a scarf, and she put on a thin underwear. Beneath her underwear, her nipples were dancing; she didn't wear a bra either. She was walking like a blonde free girl who was angry of nature and human kind.

"Oh sorry, you haven't gone to the city yet!" Rozhan said this and dropped the clothes, ran upstairs and wore a scarf then came back.

"Hello, dear Rozhan, good morning, no we won't go today."

"Haji Baxtyar came in the morning to fix our door," Fariba informed her.

"Okay, I thought he had come for something else," said Rozhan.

"Something else, Rozhan? Like what?" enquired Fariba.

"Haji Baxtyar is also so unlucky in his life. His first wife died and the second one, you know, …that's why he wants to marry again, and he is looking for an appropriate partner.

"So what?" Fariba replied, astonished.

"Maybe he came for Daya Halaw!"

Fariba burst out laughing, but Araaz flushed with anger and took Dlir and went out.

That day, Araaz and Fariba took Dlir and the puppy out for picnic to the hills behind their house.

They asked Daya Halaw to come by, but she refused and said,

"The women might come and I should stay home."

Rozhan put her head out of the window and said, "Go that way. After the cemetery, you will get to the fountain." They said good byes and left. Araaz brought Albert Camus's book. His favourite writers were Marquez and Llosa. He had a plan to write a short story, although he couldn't accomplish it, but he narrated it several times for Fariba.

"A girl was trying to write a novel. Each time she was close to finish it, a problem came up. First time, her room went on fire and her writing burned in the fire. Next time, her brother mistakenly took the book to the school and lost it there. One more time, when she finished her writing, she put it inside her father's safe, but the thief broke into their house and took the whole safe with them. As a last resort, her father bought a computer for her to type and save it. Unfortunately, at the last chapter of her typing, the lightening hit their house and her computer crashed. The girl gave up writing forever."

Fariba always told him to write it. "Why don't you write it down? Are you afraid that nobody will read it?"

Araaz answered her with a smile on his lips. It is enough for me to write that poem that made you fall in love with me.

On their honeymoon, Araaz promised Fariba to write a poem for her every night. He wouldn't know it would last for six years.

Fariba has written them all in a note book, and each night, she reads one of them as remembrance.

"You stared at Rozhan, I saw that, how you looked at her breasts!" Fariba said.

"Oh my God! When will you stop this jealousy?" Araaz smiled.

"You know that I get angry by this and you repeat it again and again."

"Sweetie, I didn't look at Rozhan at all, I swear by God."

"Also, yesterday, I noticed that how you talked to that prostitute," said Fariba.

"Who?"

"That one, whom we took the TV from her in Tabriz."

"Are you serious! She was older than my mum!"

Araaz was laughing, and he took Dlir and ran towards the fountain.

"Let's go, your mum is angry! Araaz talked to Dlir.

Dlir repeated, "Mum angly, mum angly ".

When Fariba got angry, her cheeks became red. Araaz washed his face in the fountain, "It's really cold." He trembled. He came to Fariba from the back, and suddenly he hugged her from behind. Fariba got scared and fell in to the water.

"Get off me, ugly boy," Fariba screamed.

Araaz was laughing, while Dlir and the puppy were surprised. They stared at Fariba.

"Don't do that, Araaz, I get sick, it's cold," Fariba said.

"You'll dry quickly by this hot sun, don't worry."

They sat upon a big stone under the sun. Fariba spread her shirt to dry.

"Do you promise to never cheat on me?"

Araaz smiled; he looked at Fariba and hugged her.

"Don't you know me well? You know that you are all I have in this world."

"I am afraid my brothers will find us."

"Don't worry! Nobody can find us here."

Araaz made a big fire and started frying a fish. They both liked fish, especially with hot pepper. In the afternoon, they returned towards home. When they arrived home, they saw a strange thing under the Van tree, a few women had gathered around Daya Halaw, laughing loudly and Hama was playing drum for them. Fariba looked at Araaz and smiled.

"She has given them the grass, I am sure," Fariba guessed.

Fariba was laughing and Araaz, who had Dlir in his arms, couldn't say anything.

"What do all these women do near my mum," Araaz asked, astonished.

"Nothing, this is their daily routine," Rozhan opened the window and answered.

"Mr. Araaz, my refrigerator has a harsh noise, and we have guests coming tonight. If you have a time, please take a look weather, you can fix it."

"Okay," Araaz accepted, while he was thinking about his mum and those women.

They went in his house, he put Dlir down and then were about to leave …

"Where are you going Mister? Fariba asked.

"I am going up to fix the refrigerator for Rozhan," Araaz answered.

"Wait, I am coming with you."

"This is ridiculous."

"No, I am coming with you, you won't go alone!"

They went together.

"You're welcome," Rozhan hugged Dlir and said, "Is that the puppy?"

"Yes, we choose a name for it," Araaz said.

"Name for what?" asked Rozhan.

"For the puppy, we call it Ashmol," (He looked at Fariba and smiled).

"What does it mean?"

"Ask Miss. Fariba," Araaz answered, while he was checking the refrigerator.

Fariba, who was blushing, answered quickly! "It is the title of my favourite film.

"Lady Rozhan, it is finished, I fixed it well," Araaz interrupted them.

"Thank you, Mr. Araaz,"

Suddenly, they heard a loud scream from the outside.

"What was that? What are they doing?" Araaz, Fariba and Rozhan looked out from the window. The women were running fast and screaming, each one in a different direction. Araaz went down to see what happened!

"What happened, mum?" he asked.

"Daya Halaw, who was scared beyond wits, said, "We were sitting there under the tree, suddenly a big, black snake fell down on our head."

"Oh, mum what did you do?" he whispered in her mum's ear, "I told you thousand time, not to give them from that grass."

"What has this go to do with that? I told you the snake fell on us; you are telling me not to give them the grass? Are you crazy?"

"Crazy What! You gathered twenty women and give each of them a grass cigarette. You all smoked it together under the tree, so the snake got high and fell down. Look at that poor snake, it cannot find its way to the river."

"Are you worried about me or about the snake? I was about to die!"

"Oh mum! You have made me go mad."

"You already are mad."

Hama was laughing and playing drum. Gradually, the women came back and took their shoes, and then they left.

That night, Daya Halaw didn't eat at all. She didn't even talk to anyone. She went to her room early and went to sleep. All night long she had a bad dream.

In the morning, Fariba couldn't go with Araaz, that's why Araaz went alone. He kissed Fariba and Dlir and said good bye to her mum who was awake for Morning Prayer.

-May God be with you, son! And if you can please bring me some of that …" whispered Daya Halaw.

"Okay, mum, if I can find it, I'll bring it," Araaz promised.

"This time, I won't share it with anyone, don't worry, ok, I promise."

3

Daya Halaw prayed the Morning Prayer and turned on the samovar, then she washed the teapot and poured two spoons of tea in to the teapot. She prayed and chanted with her rosary; her rosary had thirty-two pieces. With each piece, she read Tohid Sora[1] twice, and when she would count all the pieces, she would assure that the tea is ready. She poured a dark tea for herself, and rolled a mixed cigarette. The sun had risen, and she inhaled the smoke deeply and drank a sip of tea after it. The voice of Rozhan could be heard.

"What is that noise, Daya Halaw?" Fariba asked.

"I don't know, let me see!"

She called Rozhan, but no one answered her. She called again,

"What happened, Rozhan?" The door opened and Rozhan came down the stairs. She sat on the second stair and started to cry. She put her hands on her face.

"What happened, Rozhan? Why are you crying? Daya Halaw asked.

She said, "Nothing."

---

[1] Islamic term, the sora of Quran

Her mother-in-law came down after her and said, "Sorry, Daya Halaw, we woke you up!"

"Hi dear, not at all, I was awake."

"Rozhan honey, get up, let's go inside, people will hear us. It is very bad." Sabir's mum said.

"Bad! Nothing could be worse than this. When you find that the brother of your husband wants to rape you!" Rozhan said this and cried again.

"Oh my God! Don't say that."

Fariba came out with Dlir in her arms. When Dlir saw Rozhan crying, he abruptly started to cry. They took Rozhan up.

"The previous night, the mother-in-law and brother-in-law were invited to Rozhan's house. In the morning, when I was still half asleep, I noticed that a man was hugging me from behind. First, I thought, it was a dream, but then I thought, Sabir has come back. When I turned around, I saw Ali (Sabir's brother). I asked him 'what are you doing, you pig!' He got scared and ran away quickly."

"God damn him, I'll tell his father to treat him well," her mother-in-law said.

"It was nothing, just a nightmare," Daya Halaw said.

"What dream? What nightmare? It was as big as this, Rozhan pointed to an insecticide spray."

Hama looked back and said, "It is nightmare, yes nightmare."

At that time, Haji Baxtyar came out of nowhere for fixing the door.

Daya Halaw went to open the door for him.

"Hello, Miss. How are you?" Haji Baxtyar greeted her.

"Good, thanks to God, we are good," Daya Halaw answered.

"Chief Salim told me that, you are from Krmashan."

"Originally, we are from Martyr Halabja. My husband was member of Democrat party. At the time of Halabja chemical bombardment, we were separated. Me and Araaz survived and escaped to Iran. In Krmashan we had some relatives, that's why we stayed there for a while. We searched everywhere for my husband, but we couldn't find him."

"You are very welcome. Here is also your homeland."

"Thank you, Haji, these people are very nice to us."

Haji Baxtyar was busy with fixing the door, and Daya Halaw was making tea. While fixing the door, he was singing a song of Foad Ahmad[1]. He had a pleasant voice. Daya Halaw was listening to him, behind the door. Beside his good voice, he was also a skilled carpenter; he was illiterate, but very smart. He had memorized Quran in his childhood only by listening to Mullahs[2]. He liked poetry too much. He had memorized most of Qani, Haqiqi and Mawlawi[3] poems. He also was well aware of Saadi's Gullistan[4] book. When he was young, he fell in love with one of his relatives and married her immediately. He had two son. Unfortunately, during Iraqi air bombardment, he lost his wife and his elder son.

"Dear Haji, here you go," Daya Halaw brought the tea tray.

---

[1] Kurdish singer

[2] Islamic term, equal to Imam, a person who guides the people in mosque

[3] Three Kurdish poets

[4] Saadi Shirazi is a Persian poet. His famous books are *Gulistan* and *Bustan*

"Thank you, Miss. Where are the children?" Haji Baxtyar asked.

"Araaz left early in the morning and Fariba is upstairs," she answered.

"God bless them."

Daya Halaw took out his Tobacco to role a cigarette. Haji Baxtyar, who also wanted to smoke, surpassed her and took off a cigarette from his pack and said,

"Daya Halaw, here, smoke one from my pack; it is the best original Winston."

"Thank you, but I like this tobacco more."

"What is that green Tobacco?" Haji Baxtyar asked.

"Sorrow and grieve made me fully depressed. The pain in my hands and feet was about to kill me. I visited every doctor in Krmashan and Hamadan, but no use, until Araaz, God bless him, found this tobacco for me. Now I feel much better and my pain is reduced," Daya Halaw explained.

"Can I see that?" Haji Baxtyar asked.

"Here you go."

Haji, who liked to discover new things, took a little bite of it, and tasted it by his tongue, then he smelled it again.

"Do we have to always mix them, or it can be used alone?" Haji asked.

Daya Halaw lit up her cigarette and answered,

"Araaz says you have to mix them!"

"I want to try one, please! You said it is produced by Hamadan?"

"No, Araaz said Asadabad, not Hamadan. Here, you can try this."

"Yes. Asadabad, it was famous for its opium in early days."

Haji Baxtyar rolled one cigarette and said, "Let me finish my work, then I will smoke it." Daya Halaw fed the puppy and Haji completed his job gradually.

Daya Halaw stood up and looked at the door.

Thanks a lot, it is perfect.

Haji Baxtyar gathered his staff and put them in the hallway. He took his cigarette out and lit it up. Daya Halaw brought him a cup of tea.

Haji Baxtyar closed his eyes, clapped and recited a poem:

I was sick and miserable, you were cure and remedy.
I was poor and empty, you were greatest treasury

He opened his eyes and looked at Daya Halaw and around the house and recited a poem again, this time a little louder. He was high.

"I was poor …I was poor." He was on loop, in this part of the poem, and he only repeated it over and over.

"What is that sound?"

"It is downstairs; it is like someone is dancing."

Rozhan, who had just stopped crying, came down with Fariba and Dlir.

They saw Daya Halaw was standing in the entrance, and Haji Baxtyar was singing non-stop and aloud and dancing a Kurdish dance.

Fariba saw the bag of tobacco and smiled.

"Daya Halaw, what happened to Haji?" Rozhan asked.

"I don't know, he was calm a few minutes ago," Daya Halaw responded, astonished.

Haji Baxtyar ran barefoot towards the mountain behind the house, laughing his head off. He left all his stuff behind.

Rozhan looked at Fariba surprisingly and said, "All the villagers have gone crazy."

Fariba caught a bad headache. Rozhan and Daya Halaw both were giving her a head massage.

"You got colic, here," Daya Halaw said.

"Yes, I know. Yesterday, Araaz got me wet on the fountain. I told him not to do that."

Rozhan brought a pill for her, and Daya Halaw brought Mrs. Zinat.

Dlir was also a little sick.

"We have been massaging her since noon," Daya Halaw uttered.

"You are absolutely right," Miss Zinat answered.

Mrs Zinat took out a small can and said,

"This ointment is holy one. They brought it for me from Mecca. Fariba took off her clothes and Miss Zinat put her finger into the ointment.

"In the name of God, God bless you, and may give your health back to you." Miss Zinat waxed all her body while she was praying for her.

After Haji Baxtyar smoked that cigarette, he headed towards Qolqula Fountion barefoot and slept there for a while. When he woke up, he noticed that his feet had been injured. He put his feet in the fountain and washed them, then he headed towards Araaz house. When he got there, he saw some women sitting under the tree. He was hiding himself and tried to enter the house from behind, above the yard wall. The wall was very high and he was afraid to jump; because of this he jumped into the lime powder inside the yard, his whole body got covered by lime dust, then he entered the house to pick his shoes.

"Hello, anybody home?"

The entrance door was opened but nobody answered. As Haji Baxtyar went inside to take his shoes, Fariba, who woke up from the noise, saw him in this appearance and cried,

"Rozhan, the ghost, Rozhan."

Fariba passed out and Rozhan also got scared!

"It is me, Haji Baxtyar, I came to take my shoes, no need to be scared." Haji put on his shoes and left.

"Let me check on those Kojilas," said Miss Zinat and she looked inside them, "same like his wives, he has no chance in this either."

"God bless him, today he fixed our door, his voice is also so pleasant," Daya Halaw smiled.

"You are absolutely right. I remembered that his voice was pleasant when he was young. He is a wise man, and he read Quran well, but since his wife and his son, Hajar, died from the bombardment, he lost his freshness and he never was the same person. His relative gathered around to force him to marry again. He didn't agree at first, God damn Haji Basit, who found this woman for him."

"What's wrong with her, Miss Zinat?" Daya Halaw asked.

"What can I say, that woman was from Tilako village, her husband had died. She had four sons and two daughters. In the courtship ceremony, she said that she wanted nothing from Haji Baxtyar, but her sons had some debts, they wanted Haji to pay off. Haji, who was in love, accepted to pay back the debts. They got married then. They had a good relationship for a while, but suddenly, she left the house and returned to her son's house. Haji Baxtyar picked Haji Basit, and went after her. When they got there and asked for the reason, one of her sons answered that 'my mum is like an artist, if she only makes a carpet here, she could make a lot of money.'

"Your mother doesn't know anything about carpet," Haji Baxtyar retorted.

"Not at this point, although she would learn in two months," her elder son answered, and now the people said that your mother got married with no jewellery, no nothing …This time Haji Baxtyar agreed to buy her some jewellery, and because of the jewellery the problem has been solved for a while.

After a while, Haji Baxtyar wanted to visit her sister in Sullymani. He stayed there for a few days. He bought many gifts for his wife and her sons. When he came back, he saw that his wife wasn't home again. Haji's son, Sirwan told his father that the day after his departure, one of her son came by and took her. Once again, he accompanied Haji Basit and went after her.

"How will we get there in this winter?"

Despite of all the problems, they got to her oldest daughter's house. This time, they wanted something more from Haji Baxtyar. They said that, "Haji has got so many farms and money, what has he given our mother? Nothing …"

Although he got tired of all these, he promised to give her a small farm. After receiving this expensive gift, his wife came back again. Unfortunately, it didn't last long. One day, the police officer came to Haji Baxtyar and said, "You have to come with us! Someone sued you." He took Haji to the police office.

The police officer told him that your daughter's kid has taken some clothes and didn't pay for that? She had the signature of Haji and she said that in case of, I don't pay, Haji Baxtyar would be in charge.

Haji Baxtyar got really confused and said,

"The whole village knows that I have no daughter!"

A fight happened in the police office; Haji had been arrested that day. The next day, they found out that the girl was not Haji's daughter, but a daughter of his new wife. Haji, again, for the sake of his wife, payed out the debt and the issue was solved.

In the spring time, the two daughters of Haji's wife came to visit her mother, and they stayed for two months. After these two months, when they wanted to go back, Haji's wife wanted Haji's permission to go with them. Poor Haji even, bought many gifts for them and sent her back to her son's house.

Two weeks passed, and there was no sign of his wife. Haji called her sons several times, but they didn't answer him at all. After one month, he went to Haji Basit again.

"Don't say anything. Her sons called me and they said, their mum won't come back," Haji Basit informed him.

"What happened this time?"

They went after her again. But this time, when they arrived there, every one ignored them.

"This is ridiculous!" Haji Basit said.

Their elder son-in-low replied,

"Haji, our mum is very important for us, but in Haji's house, they disrespected her too much. That house is so small and with Haji's son and his bride, our mum is not free and relaxed. That house is not enough for both families.

Haji Baxtyar got angry and stood up and said, "Let's go, it is impossible, she has made up her mind." They left without saying goodbye and that was his last resort. Although after a while, one of the daughters of that woman, along with her family, came to Haji Baxtyar ask for forgiveness, but this time Haji ignored them. He even didn't open the door for them. They got divorced and Haji was free again.

4

"Why hasn't Araaz come back yet? It is late," Fariba asked Daya Halaw.

"He'll be back soon, don't worry," Daya Halaw assured her.

"He even doesn't answer his phone, I am afraid something bad has happened."

"Nothing will happen to him, don't move! Just tell me what do you want?"

"Put another blanket on me. It is cold."

"Okay."

Fariba was shivering.

"Daya Halaw, there is a sound, see if it's him."

"No, it's Rozhan, she has brought Dlir back."

"Hello, Daya Halaw, how is Fariba?" Rozhan asked.

"Sorry Rozhan, we bother you so much," Daya Halaw said.

Rozhan Rolled Dlir in a blanket.

"Dlir is also not feeling so good. He had fever, anyway I have put him to sleep," Rozhan said.

"Thank you so much!"

Daya Halaw cooked lentil soup. She poured three bowls and sat the table.

"Come, dear Rozhan, eat with us, it is hot and delicious."

Fariba was trembling under the blanket. She asked Rozhan to dial Araaz's number. Daya Halaw poured a little milk for Ashmol.

"His phone is off," Rozhan answered.

Suddenly, Fariba stood up fast, and like a crazy one, looked at the window and said,

"*In this all-limitless darkness, I only have one spark of light, so where is my spark?*

No star sparkle put an end to my darkness, please come back soon!"

Rozhan hugged her with dull tears in her eyes; duller than the flood story.

Daya Halaw recited Quran with a quiet voice and said, "He will come back soon."

Loneliness like a strange fog, had come to their house, like an uninvited guest. It was pressing her heart inside the wall. For a minute, she illustrated her misery, then she thought about the stress of being a woman and a mother.

Daya Halaw was silent, she was staring at her rosary. Ashmol finished her milk and looked at Fariba. Her shivering was decreasing gradually and her red cheeks, would reveal the incoming deadly fever. As she remembered a time that Araaz was in jail, her tears started dancing on her pink cheeks.

Rozhan put her hands on Fariba's forehead.

"You have fever."

She took off the blanket from Fariba.

Daya Halaw brought a pan of cold water, and cooled Fariba's feet with a towel.

"Rozhan, please take a look at my phone! In case somebody calls me. I put it on silent mood," Fariba asked.

"Oh, a number has called you four times, see if it is Araaz."

She took the phone from Rozhan.

"Where, who might be? Maybe, he is in a hospital."

"What hospital? What did you say? Don't worry, they'll call again," Rozhan said.

They were talking about this when the phone rang.

"Hello, why don't you answer the phone, Fariba. It is me Araaz. I was arrested around Miandowow. I am in police office now, tomorrow they'll take me to the court."

"Dear Araaz, where are you, for God's sake, I am about to get crazy!" Fariba said.

"Don't cry, my wealth, they took my phone, so I couldn't call, don't cry please, you are making me sad. How are you? How is Dlir and mum?"

"I won't let you go alone next time."

"Okay, we'll talk about this later. They'll release me, tomorrow or maybe the day after. Give the phone to mum, I want to talk to her."

He greeted his mum, and he told her to take care of Dlir and Fariba.

"Wait, Daya Halaw, I want to have a word with him."

Fariba grabbed the phone and said, "I cannot live without you, please come back soon."

"I'll be back soon, kiss you, goodbye, I have to go."

Fariba languished like a fire that goes out under the water. She put the phone to her heart and looked at the moonlight, a few drops of tears were coming down from her eyes, heading towards the vague valley of her cheeks.

"Did she sleep?" asked Rozhan.

"Yes, thank God!"

"Daya Halaw! If she wakes up again, give her one of these pills."

"Okay, dear Rozhan, thank you very much, you helped much."

5

"Thank you, brother, thank you so much!"

"Let it be between us, unless it causes me a big problem. Prisoners are not allowed to have a phone call, but I helped you, because you are Kurdish! Get back inside, tomorrow they will take you to the Mahabad court. I hope a kind judge will consider your case."

Araaz gave his phone back, and thanked him again. He was from Bokan, and that night, he was the chief prison guards. Most of prisoners were Turkish, they gave Araaz a pillow and one blanket. He went inside and sat in a corner. Araaz was exhausted, but he couldn't sleep. That morning, like always, he was standing in bazar. There was no cargo for him, he was pothering around and aimlessly, he headed towards the cafe street, a dusty, sad street. The smoke of hookah and cigarette along with the dust made the street dark and sad. Two electric poles had surrounded the street. Most of the house of that street had two floors. The first floor was reserved for shop. There were only two restaurants there, and the rest of the store were cafe! Under the shadow of a big walnut tree, there were a few wooden old-fashioned tables and chairs. Some people were sitting around the tables. Two young guys were talking about the last night fight in the street, the fight of two kids was about to make a big problem. On the other table, an old man was sitting with a walnut in his hand, and a cup of tea was there in front of him on the table. He was staring at the bunch of ducks swimming in the river.

The river divided the city into two parts at that time of the year – the river was empty. He was waiting patiently with grief for autumn's coming. Although he knew that for river rebirth, he couldn't build all his hope on autumn's coming. Oh history, Oh misery, Oh Kurdistan. Since the beginning of the history, Kurdistan and misery have been inseparable twins, or better to say that history presented Kurdistan the gift of misery frequently.

"Please pour me a cup of tea!" His cigarette finished between his finger; he drank a sip of his tea.

A man had spread a nylon underlay in front of the Cafe. He had put some different books on the underlay for sale. Nowadays, nobody buys a book! Even in the university, I wonder, if this poor man wants to find a customer here? Araaz looked at his book reluctantly.

"Why do you look at me like that? You think I am crazy!" the book seller asked.

"No, no, of course not, but to whom you want to sell your book in this dusty street?"

"Ha ha! Don't worry, here you can find a real customer."

There were some Kurdish books like Cheshti Mjiwr [1] and Dark & Bright, some novels by Shirzad Hasan and Ata Nahaee[2] and some Russian famous novels. There was also *Freedom or Death of Kazantzakis.*

---

[1] A book by Hazhar mukryani
[2] Two famous kurdish novelist

A little further, there were sounds of greeting between some young guys drowned in the harsh screaming of a fish monger, who was sitting in his car and shouted 'fish come here, fresh fish'.

"Hello Mr. Jalal, I have been waiting for you for a long time, how is Kak[1] Ahmad?"

The book seller welcomed Jalal.

"It has been two days since the border was closed. We needed some stuff. I thought it is the right time to come to see you, too."

Jalal was a thin guy with a sparkling eyes and black long hair; his long, black ponytail hair made him appear manly.

"Kak Ahmad is good, his eyesight has begun to fail."

Apposite to Jalal, the book seller was a big-bellied, fat man, who could hardly fasten the last button of his shirt. He was almost bald.

"Did you bring me the books?"

The voice of fish monger became louder and harsher. The bookseller secretly glanced at Araaz and took off two books and rolled them in a newspaper. Then he put it inside a black bag and handed it to Jalal and sent him away. It seemed that the book seller was afraid of Araaz.

"Jalal is a Kolbar. He graduated from university, but unfortunately, he couldn't find a good job.

"God bless Kak Ahmad who found a job for Jalal. He is such a smart guy."

---

[1] Kak is a kurdish title, approximately equal to sir or Mr. in English. It means brother in kurdish

Araaz lifted the books and took a short look at the first and second pages, then he put it back in its places. He had read many of them.

"What do you read? I mean literature, philosophy?"

"I read novel mostly."

The book seller scratched his belly and gave Araaz, *The Brothers Karamazov* novel.

"This is wow, this is the real novel."

Araaz took the book from his hand, and unwillingly put it back and said,

"Middle Eastern people, always like to give advice."

"This is a real novel."

"But Russian writers like advice, Kafka, Camus and Marquez are real novelist!"

Araaz found a book of Abdulla Ocalan.[1]

"Isn't this book illegal?"

"Ha-ha I am illegal, you are illegal!"

While he was cleaning his hand's wound infection with a white hand kerchief, he waited until the screams of the fish monger and the crowing of a bunch of crows on the top of the nearby sycamore stopped, then he continued,

---

[1] Abdullah Ocalan, also known as Apo is the modern leader of Kurdistan Workers Party (PKK). He is regarded by millions of Kurds as their political leader and new hope for their rights. He is a great thinker and intellectual figure of Middle east. In 1999, Ocalan was captured in Nairobi, and Turkey has sent him to jail. He has written many books, including; *Democratization in Turkey, and solution to the Kurdish Question, Democratic* Confederalism.

"These people in the street, these crows, that fish monger, even the voices are illegal. Sometimes I think that our homeland is illegal for us!"

The bookseller scratched his head for a while and patted his forehead, then he took out a green wool hat from his pocket, whipped the dust of it and put it on.

"Do you know why I spread my books here, near the river?"

He didn't allow Araaz to respond and continued,

"Because I like flood, a merciless flood that breaks the bridges, washes the dirt, squeezes the throat of betrayal and disloyalty, and then at the end it challenges death! I am waiting for that flood."

"Why death?"

"Because the purest word in this world is death, death from hunger, death for liberty, for honour, for truth!"

"Death is free in itself."

Suddenly Araaz stood up, just like a person who got electrocuted, and stared at the first page of one of the books. 'Sanandaj, Palestine Street, and his signature was underlined. He was shocked, his hand was trembling. He took out his cigarette and lit a cigarette. Araaz opened the book and smelled it. He drew his hand on the lines of the book. He was sure that it was his own book; he was about to fall.

"What happened to you, sir?" the bookseller asked.

"Where did you get this book?" Araaz asked.

"Why?"

"It is my book. A few years ago, they forcibly entered my house and took it away with some other books!" Araaz was holding his face with both hands, the bookseller hugged Araaz and leaned him against the wall, and brought him a glass of water.

"An Ilamian guy sends the books to me from Tehran."

"I was studying politics in Krmashan University. My thesis was about the history of socialism in Kurdistan, more about the differences between Qasemlu and Ocalan's socialism.

"They were against me. They told me that this topic is forbidden.

"They warned me not to talk about these two persons, but I made up my mind, until the day of presentation. I was about to start my introduction when suddenly some men came out of nowhere, and interrupted the session and captured me in front of my professors. They also investigated my house and took away my computer and all my books. I stayed in prison for some days, then they took me to the court. In the court, the judge called my name. He spoke Persian but it was obvious, that he was Kurdish. With his angry look, the judge could break down all innocent or guilty spirits. Any of my answers to the judge's questions could dig my grave easily.

"It is obvious that you know Qasemlu and Ocalan and their socialism well, and you also believe in them," the judge asked me.

"No, I believe in myself."

"Ha ha! Yourself, it is written here that you are from Halabja, you are not from here," the judge looked at the papers under his hand.

"What do you mean by 'here'?"

"I mean Iran, you are from Iraq! Is that clear?"

"It doesn't make any difference for me, I spoke Kurdish in Halabja, here I also speak Kurdish. I wear Kurdish clothes in both places. I don't know anything about your borders. My father has been lost in Iran and my mother escaped from the bombardment of Saddam Hussein. I am the offspring of my father's disappearance and my mother's asylum."

Suddenly, the judge shocked me with a loud noise, while he was bonging his fist on the table.

"Silence! Being Kurdish is different from being Kurdistanian. Being Kurdish in not a crime, but the idea of great Kurdistan is poisonous. These are red lines. In Iran, you can live as an Iranian Kurd. If you don't like it, you can leave here!"

I couldn't sit on the chair because of my backache. The torture of past two days had exhausted me, completely.

"Which party pays you? Which country do you work for? Tell me!"

"I am not working for any group or party. I just did a research about two Kurdish leaders, nothing more!"

"Research! Ha ha, what is your goal?"

"I don't have any special goal, it is only one research."

It was clear that the judge doesn't know anything about socialism, or about Qasemlu and Ocalan.

"Your house was full of illegal books. Only on the possession of those books alone I can send you to jail for ten years."

"How did you get out of there?" the bookseller asked.

"I was imprisoned for a year and expelled from the university."

In the middle of this conversation, Araaz's phone rang.

"Sorry, sir, I have to go, and how much is the book?" Araaz asked.

"It is free for you; it is your book."

Araaz accepted and said goodbye to the bookseller and then left.

I wish that, in one of my dreams, the depth of a black sea would swallow every hour of life in this land, then a small red fish would give all these hours of suffering to the fishes of the sea as a gift. The sorrow behind the minutes. I wonder, for which disaster, the fishes would cry: motherland, hunger or a blind love!

On the way to Miandowow, Araaz was only thinking about his book.

In the car, he was listening to Najmadin Xolam's[1] song, when the police stopped and arrested him.

"Sorry, officer, I want to tell you something important," Araaz begged.

"Say it."

"There is a book in the car that is illegal, if you please …"

"Don't worry, I hid it before you said it," the officer assured him.

After serving his lunch, Araaz took a walk inside the Mahabad city.

He went to Bodagh sultan and visited the graves of Qazi.

Mohammed, Hemn and Hazhar[2]! Araaz parked his car in a street, and walked to Azadi square. Fariba wanted some green cotton and a pair of ankle bracelet. Araaz bought the things for Fariba. He went around, until he got to Chwarchra[3] and Soor mosque, He could smell the emptiness of the streets.

---

[1] Kurdish singer

[2] Kurdish writers and poets

[3] A famous square and region in Mahabad city. The great Qazi Mohammad was hanged in Chwarchra Square.

He circled around until he arrived at Hersh Lalosh's book store. Inside the bookstore, Hersh was presenting *Animal Farm* ta a young girl; *"Court of life, Prison of Thought, die for bread, Running towards a hug full of love* ….

The August sun was mildly warm; Araaz entered Mikaeel garden, and sat under the shade of a willow tree and lit up his last cigarette.

"How many summers and springs should pass, how many clouds and how much rains, earthquakes and floods should flow and how many bombardments and execution remain, until this land get free."

"Blood pool, Martyr's body, Martyr's son, Martyr's mother."

"Would you polish your shoes, sir?"

"Ice cream, Kim ice cream, buy one get one free."

"Fresh popcorn, come here!"

I wish someone would come and say, fresh thought, new idea instead of ice cream and polish, or another one says, cold mastaw[1] and the other have an arm full of narcissus flower of Qandil Mountain.

"No comrade, my shoes are not polish type and don't like ice cream either."

A boy and a girl were sitting on the grass, had their backs to a fir tree in the park. The boy put his hand around girl's neck, and he was kissing her from time to time. Their laughter created a beautiful feeling, even the trees were radiant, just like a small piece of freedom had been revealed. The girl and boy in their youth, full of passion and love! A little farther, a man on a cart was selling tea.

---

[1] Kind of cold drinking, composed of yogurt and water

"Please pour me a cup of tea."

There was a furry and two police man stopped the young boy and his girlfriend.

"Please, a strong tea! Do you have a cigarette?"

"What are you doing here? What is your relationship with this girl?"

It was clear that blooming of this little amount of freedom can make opponents angry. Amorous laughter, a few kisses and hugs are forbidden and illegal. Kiss, hug and laughter in the cry, torture and execution land …how dare you talk about these … they were scared much.

"What kind of cigarette do you want?"

"Please officer! …."

"I don't have red Winston, smoke the white, it is even better."

"Why don't you say something, you have to come with us to the manner police office."

"The girl started crying, the tea seller was laughing."

"Please officer, if our father knows, he will kill us."

In the midst of this conversation, the boy said,

"We didn't do anything wrong; we were just talking.

"Ha ha! What more did you want to do?" Police said.

"We only wanted to know each other more."

"Their sheepish, apology …."

"I wanted to explain to judge that the history made me to put my life in danger for a loaf of bread!" said by Araaz.

In the gas station, a fight happened. A person shouted, "You bustard winked at my wife! You violated my honour."

"Winked! I wonder how fragile; Honour is that it could be broken by an eye winking."

We have been told that mother land is our honour, and we are silent, they took our land and break our collective honour.

Ha ha Honour.

"Let it be the last time. This time I won't confiscate your car and I will ignore it. You will go to the jail if you do it again," judge warned me.

I wanted to say, "Dear judge, I have been in jail for a long time, this is not new for me. I wonder if someone will give me the glad tiding of Freedom."

I wanted to inform that stupid tea seller that life is waking up early in the morning, before us, and after serving its coffee, it starts to watch and mock us all.

Last night in prison, after a few years, I saw a dream of my father.

In my dream, we replaced each other. I was his father and he was my son.

"Dad, today our teacher read a Sherko Bikas[1] poem."

"The whore, those who tell me ...."

"These books are illegal bro!"

"Thank you so much, you saved my life!"

"These will stay with me. I will give you my number, whenever you come to Bokan, just call me. I will bring the books back."

"Yes, my sweetie. I am about to depart, and don't worry, I will drive safe.

Fariba was calling again and again.

---

[1] Modern Kurdish poet, who widely regarded as the greatest Kurdish national poet

"Son! This poem is not by Sherko Bikas. It is Pashiw's[1] poem."

"The teacher told me they replaced too."

"Thank you, judge."

I stood up to leave the court when the judge told me, "Only because you are from Halabja." I looked back and said nothing. If I could rewind the movie of life, or Saddam Hussein would have been a little kinder, and hadn't bombed Halabja, what would the judge have said then?

I wanted to explain for the judge that for us, every day is Halabja, haven't they seen our hunger?

Araaz stopped the car in Bokan to buy some hot pepper,

"Please give me two fishes and please put some ice on it, because I have a long way to my home." He took his books back from the Bucanion solider.

"Oh, my dad, Kak Ahmad, I wish, I knew, where you are now! And what you are doing. Not that I missed you, no, because even that time in Halabja, you were the son of your party, and we were nothing to you."

Someone say that he has been lost, when he was looking for Araaz and Daya Halaw. Nobody has seen him, even none of his comrades. They told me that they searched everywhere for him. The only clue was that Kak Ahmad was the only person, who was in the middle of the negotiation between Qasemlu and the Islamic regime. Kak Ahmad was the only trustable member of party. After the Vienna terror, nobody saw Kak Ahmad. I wanted to say but all of my life was passed in these all hesitates to say, so I said nothing at the end!!

---

[1] Contemporary Kurdish poet and writer

6

"Thank you, Rozhan, why did you bring food again? Daya Halaw has made a pot of lentils soup," Fariba said.

"Don't say that, it is boiled chicken. I put onion and pepper in it. It is great for your sickness. How is Dlir?" Rozhan asked.

"He is not good at all. Last night, he didn't sleep a bit, his whole body has red freckles. I thought he had been bitten by an insect, but Daya Halaw says it is measles!"

"Oh my God, his whole face is also affected, we have to take him to hospital. Let's go."

"No, Rozhan, I don't want to bother you anymore, I am waiting for Araaz."

"Let's go and don't say anything more, because the doctor wouldn't be there in the afternoon, hurry up."

They tightened Dlir's clothes and went to the clinic.

"I don't think that the doctor could visit you today. He is so busy," the secretary said.

"This kid is very sick."

Dlir was sweaty, and Fariba had a dry cough. Daya Halaw was praying as always.

"Wait, let me check if I could send you in," the secretary said.

"Miss Rozhan, do you have any medical insurance?" the secretary asked.

"I have, but they don't have any," Rozhan answered.

"Go inside, after Malazhn[1]," the secretory said.

"Give them my turn, too, my case is not emergency," Malazhn offered.

"Thank you so much," Rozhan said and they entered the doctor's room.

The doctor was so rude. He didn't take her eyes off Rozhan.

"How old is he?" Doctor asked.

"He is almost two years old."

"Has he been vaccinated?"

"No."

"It might be measles! I prescribed a syrup for him, give him three times a day. If he won't get better, bring him again tomorrow."

"Hello Daya Halaw, I am Aftaw, wife of the Imam of mosque, and sister of Haji Baxtyar."

"Hello Miss Aftaw, how are you?" Daya Halaw greeted her.

"Haji Baxtyar says so many good things about you. Unfortunately, we haven't met yet. It is so good to see you, now."

"God bless Haji Baxtyar, we bother Haji so much."

"Don't say that, you are our guest, we have to serve you more. Haji is poor, and bad luck one. He lost his first wife and elder son in the bombardment. His second wife was a Satan. God liked Haji Baxtyar and save him from that Satan."

---

[1] Wife of mullah is called Malazhn

"I also prescribed two ampoules and a cough syrup for you."

"Thank you, doctor."

When they were on their way out, the doctor wrote his mobile number on a small piece of paper and gave it to Rozhan. Rozhan took it and tore it apart in front of him.

"Rude baldhead," Rozhan told the doctor and went out. She shut the door firmly.

"We wanted to come to your house with Imam and Chief Salim and also, we want to talk with Mr. Araaz. Unofficially, Malazhn proposed to Daya Halaw.

"I don't know, Malazhn. I have only this son; besides, I am not in a good mood lately. I am not young enough for—"

"Don't say that, you are not old, and you cannot stay with your son and bride forever. Haji Baxtyar is also alone just like you."

"Why are you angry?" Fariba asked Rozhan.

"That rude, bald head, bastard! His eyes were on my breast at all times."

"Let's go, Daya Halaw," Rozhan said.

"Thank you, Malazhn, you have been so kind to us!" Daya Halaw said.

On their way home, they were talking all about the rudeness of the doctor.

That bastard didn't look at Dlir at all, his eyes were on me all the time!" Rozhan complained.

Daya Halaw was thinking about Malazhn's words and said nothing.

"Hey, girls," Daya Halaw broke the silence, and said, "do not make fun of me, please, I want to say something. That woman in the hospital, I mean Malazhn, proposed to me!

"I was wondering why she gave us her turn, now I understand why," Rozhan said.

"What did you say, Daya Halaw?" Fariba asked.

"What could I say? I said that I have a great son and bride, although I don't want to impose on you anymore."

"Why you say that, Daya, you know that me and Araaz like to be with you forever, and you are so respectable for us." Fariba told her, then she called Araaz.

"Haji Baxtyar is a good man, Daya Halaw," Rozhan added this point.

"Where are you, Araaz?" Fariba asked.

"Don't tell anything to Araaz, Fariba!" Daya Halaw begged.

"Don't worry, Daya."

"What should I tell Araaz? I want to marry in this age!" Daya Halaw repeated this several times.

"Don't worry about that, Daya. I can handle it," Fariba assured her again.

"When will they come?"

"She didn't determine the date, but she said we have a plan to come with Chief Salim's family."

For that lunch, Miss Zinat was invited to her son's house. Her son, Keywan, was Araaz's neighbour. After the lunch, Miss Zinat couldn't wait to see Daya Halaw, and went to Daya Halaw's hangout.

"How are your son and bride? Are they okay?" Daya Halaw welcomed Miss Zinat.

"What can I say? They are not good, my poor boy studied so hard, until he became a teacher, but he got fired. Someone ratted him out and they expelled him."

"What was that?"

"They said that Keywan was a member of Komala[1] party. They came and took him from the school. God had mercy they didn't execute him, and now he is doing Kolbari. His wife is also sick."

Daya Halaw informed Miss Zinat about Haji Baxtyar's proposal.

"You are absolutely right, I don't know, Haji Baxtyar …"

Miss Zinat was not finished, when Fariba screamed. "Help, Daya help me!"

"What happened?"

"Come here. Dlir, Dlir."

"Oh my God, what happened to Dlir," Daya Halaw asked and ran inside. She saw Fariba was crying.

"Don't cry, be quiet!"

"Dlir is dying, he is not breathing."

Dlir was silent and breathless, like a piece of meat. No matter how hard Daya Halaw and Miss Zinat tried and massaged him, it was useless. Fariba and Rozhan were crying together."

"Hurry up, Rozhan, go and find some flour for me," Daya Halaw ordered.

"I have some, I will bring it in no time," Rozhan answered and went up.

"And you, Fariba, you go and heat a pan of water."

"Miss Zinat, please make a prefect Niwanmak[2] (complex of flour and salt).

They made Niwanmak, took off Dlir's clothes and put him inside the pan of Niwanmak. The flour and salt complex

---

[1] Kurdish armed party, that fight against the Islamic regime of Iran
[2] Kurdish remedy consist of water, salt and flour

covered Dlir's whole body, except for his eyes. They all sat and started praying for him.

"We have to take him to the city hospital."

"How could we take him; he is not even breathing."

Fariba was praying with tears in her eyes, like the time Araaz was in jail, and she was sitting near the window and praying for him, until the sun was setting. Like the day her brothers forced her to marry.

"I loved him and I will love him forever."

She remembered that day. She couldn't do anything, except for crying and praying. It seemed that measles had conquered the whole of Dlir's body. He had scratched his face so much that it was bloody!

"Unfortunately, we couldn't vaccinate him."

Death, like a fearless guest, was sitting above the room.

"Hey, lady, bring me a cup of tea!"

Death, stretched its legs and lit a Cuban cigarette and poured its ashes in to the pan and giggled from time to time. It puffed the smoke on the owner's face. The owner of the house had been disarmed. Like her ancestors, hundreds of years ago, she wanted to save her son by this remedy. It was like this and it will remain like this, old and new. Life and death are correlative. Death is a part of life; it is not the end of it.

"Rozhan, please open the door for Hama!" Daya Halaw asked Rozhan to answer Hama.

"What happened, Hama?" Rozhan asked.

"I am afraid of this dog, she doesn't let me in."

Rozhan grabbed Hama's hand and took him upstairs.

Silence filled the room, fear danced in the death banquet. Everyone was waiting for the destiny to ignore the reality of death and postponed it.

Dlir was the result of a fiery love, he was the child of fearless lover's story.

In the near future, he would supposed to retell the love story of his parents for the child in the school. For the children who are not familiar with love, the children of coldness and betrayal era …Dlir opened his eyes; he couldn't cry, but he stared at her mother who was staring at the windows.

The puppy (Ashmol) went inside. She was standing next to the remedy pan, and licked Dlir's body. She wanted to get closer to Dlir, but her foot got stuck in the paste pan. Ashmol started to bark, calling for help. Dlir laughed at Ashmol. Fariba heard Ashmol's bark and went for help. She saw Dlir was laughing at Ashmol.

Fariba shouted aloud, "Daya Halaw, Rozhan, come here Dlir …Dlir!"

Fariba took Dlir out of the pan of paste and cried, "Thank God he is a live!"

Daya Halaw hugged Dlir and kissed him. That day, they all saw death for more than an hour. The death came bitterly, without greeting and left without a goodbye!

"Come, Rozhan!"

"Hello, Araaz, where are you? You said 'I am in Saggz an hour ago, you have to be here now."

7

"It is not her fault, what can she do?" Fariba warned Araaz, not to tell anything to Daya Halaw.

"What proposal? I don't understand, why does she want to marry again?"

"What did your mother see in your father? He was just a faraway shadow. That poor woman has not experienced any happiness in this world. She is getting old."

"What do you expect from me? Do you want me to celebrate, ha? Do I need to be happy, because my mum wants to get married again at this age?"

"She also needs someone who can be patient with her, talk to her and fill up her loneliness! Ok enough with the frown! Is it beautiful?"

Fariba pointed to her ankle bracelet.

"Yes, it is so beautiful."

"I will also knit a yarn scarf for you."

"Why a scarf?"

"Because in winter you get sick quickly. I will make a long scarf for you, Mr. Araaz!"

"You are just like my mother, we are in the middle of summer, but you are worried about winter!"

Fariba was busy treating one acne on Araaz's shoulder with both hands.

"The judge took pity on me, he said that because I am from Halabja, he would let it go this time."

"But why did he take pity on you? You didn't do anything wrong," Fariba complained.

"Fariba! Why was your face covered in powder, when I came inside."

"Your mother can't sleep. I see her light is still on."

"Did you bake in the clay oven?"

"What oven?"

"Dlir was also powdered, all his body!"

"I'll knit the scarf in a few days."

"Miss Zinat was also heavily powdered!"

"The ankle bracelet is so beautiful. I would have been happier if you had bought a nose ring too, was that expensive?"

"Hama had a handful of bread dough in his hand, did you bake Kolira[1]?"

"Doesn't that bastard know that this people have no other jobs!"

"Ashmol also was licking the bread dough around her mouth."

"Aren't they going to give you back the TVs? Are they?"

"There was a pan of bread dough in the yard and Rozhan was busy cleaning it!"

"The doctor injected me with two ampoules today, I was about to die! Is that nothing to you? You don't care about your wife?"

---

[1] A Kurdish thick bread

As he heard Fariba's words, he threw the blanket away and got up.

"Sweetie, tell me what happened. Why ampoule? Why don't you tell me, what happened here?"

"Quiet, Dlir is sleeping. Let me tell you, Araaz. Today, Dlir almost died and came alive again!!"

"What does that mean? Enlighten me!"

"Dlir got measles! This morning, we took him to a doctor. The doctor said that, because he hasn't been vaccinated, he has been infected strongly. When we returned home, his body was completely cold, and he didn't move at all. Your mum put him in the Niwanmak and Thank God he came alive again after one hour!"

Araaz stood up and took a cigarette out of his pocket and went outside.

Daya Halaw was sitting there with a cigarette in her hard.

"Why don't you sleep mum?"

"I cannot sleep, son, I was thinking about Haji Baxtyar's request."

"Yes, Fariba has told me."

"I don't want to leave you. You might be thinking that how can a woman in my age get married again, or you may think, that how can I forget your father ….?"

"Mum."

"Wait, my son, you know better than me, that your father has been lost for several years, and I don't want to be a burden to you anymore."

"Ok, mum, it is up to you, and we will respect your decision."

8

The mountain was announcing the arrival of autumn to the forest and lovers. It was end of August. The September was haunted by the magic of fall. The wind has turned the sky in to its dance stage and every now and then was striking the breast of earth, leaves were ready to dance, colours were waiting for the earth's magic symphony, to turn into rainbow and sing the autumn song for the lovers!

Autumn was the season that Araaz and Fariba for the first time, and promised each other to be together forever in eternal love …

"14th of October was our first date, I remember your poem Mr. Araaz."

"I have been waiting for you, for a long time."

In our last meeting
Crazy me in a limitless euphoria, became a lovelorn of your magic eyes
My Fall, you are late
I have been lost without you
You, again back and see me My arms are open like a mendicant you came, me dancing in the Fall
Yellow

Oh moonlight, mirror and water I see all your beauty, all Autumn beauty
In her eyes.

"Araaz, why did you persist to marry me?"

"When I was a child, I wished to shoot a stone into the heart of the sky with a bow."

"After those all problems, why didn't you leave me?"

"I wanted to hit that star that tormented the other little stars."

"I almost died when my sister, Asrin, told me that you went to another girl." That day, all the world died to me.

-Hit its heart and free the little stars.

I said Araaz, "Do you think that our new Pomegranate tree will grow?"

Those little stars would challenge, the darkness in the sorrow land.

I wonder, if our first Pomegranate tree, has got any fruits.

"I had a dream. In my dream, I don't know when, in a farm full of Autumn, Jalal Malak Sha [1] was giving Pomegranate to everyone as a gift. When he got to me, he said nothing and passed. I said, 'what about me?' He didn't give me any Pomegranate. A few days later, he wrote me a letter, 'all the Pomegranates are yours.'

No sweetie, it wasn't my first poem.
Your love smelled like an Autumn Apple,
Mad and crazy
Full of hope

---

[1] Kurdish poets, writer from Rozhhalat (east Kurdistan), Sna city.

Eager of the first kiss of rain My breath, look at the loneliness of the street,

My poem was waiting for you

Oh, queen of my heart to catch the whiteness of your eyes, I dispatched the heart of darkness

But you didn't come

The fight between dawn and horizon came to end still, you didn't come I am going to my end waiting for you

Oh, queen of my heart!!

9

After Araaz and Daya Halaw accepted his proposal, Haji Baxtyar insisted on having ceremony.

"What ceremony? Your ages are not appropriate for such a thing," Chief Salim said.

"This man is crazy," Imam said, agreeing with Chief.

"People will make fun of us," Haji Baxtyar's sister repeated.

"What are you talking about? I will hold a ceremony at any cost, it's settled then."

Chief Salim took a look at Imam and said,

"Ok, whatever you like, let's go Aftaw."

Imam and Chief Salim along with their wives, left Haji Baxtyar's house. Haji Baxtyar also came out with them and said,

"I am going too, I have to go to the town tomorrow."

Araaz was warming up his car. It rained that night till the morning. Like the willows tree by the river, the leaves of the van tree were turning to yellow. The weather was cold and it was raining a lot. The smell of rain and soil were mixed with the roar of the river, the sun also showed up itself with grace and charm.

"Fariba, hurry up. It's getting late," Araaz repeated again.

The rain had stopped and the sun was shining, but a dark cloud from the west was moving towards them, although Israel Radio station had predicted a heavy rain, but Haji Baxtyar was refusing to accept this news and prediction about the weather. He believed that all these news were false.

"When have they told the truth?" For the first time, Haji accused Israel Radio station of being liar, or maybe, Haji wanted to deceive himself.

"Araaz look, it is Haji Baxtyar, I think he is waiting for a taxi," Fariba said.

"I know, ignore him," Araaz answered.

"How can we ignore him? Shame on you!" Araaz reluctantly stopped the car for Haji Baxtyar.

"Where do you go Haji?" Araaz asked and Haji got in the car, without answering him, since Haji also wants to go to the town, Araaz gave him a ride.

On the way, Haji was talking about the ceremony, preparing the chef and music group.

"Why are you making it so complicated? We are only fourteen people, we cook our own food, we don't need a chef."

"No, Mr. Araaz, I invited all my friends and relatives."

"How can we hold ceremony in this rain? The flood will take us away!"

"It will stop, don't worry, although I prepared a safe place, near the Van tree by the river for bride and groom."

Haji prepared everything, but the rain did not stop. It rained heavily for a whole week; the river rebirthed again. Elders of the village were not so excited about that, they thought that a disaster would happen. Haji Baxtyar was sad and angry.

"It has been raining for three days, please enough with the rain!" Haji complained.

His sister wanted to cheer him up and said, "This amount of raining is not sufficing; earth is still thirsty." These remarks made Haji angrier.

"It will stop, don't worry, Baxtyar," Aftaw reassured him.

Suddenly, Haji Baxtyar got an idea; he remembered his old friend, Haji Basit. Haji Baxtyar went to him to solve this problem.

"Why don't you go to Imam and your sister?" Basit asked.

"Listen to me, Basit. Your problem with Imam Abeed is not related to me, you know that I was on your side in that case, besides, this problem goes back thirty years; let it go please, let it go, enough!"

"Enough what? That bastard deceived me and took your sister Aftaw from me. Imam Abeed sent an asshole to your father, just to talk shit about me. He turned Aftaw against me and this is my life, you see! No wife, no children, no nothing. Even now, he sometimes creates some rumours about me on having gay relationships. God damn you, Abeed!" Haji Basit blushed, his problem with Imam Abeed was about Haji Baxtyar's sister. They both wanted Aftaw.

"It was your fault as well, you said that he was a thief. You insulted him too."

"You know that he was a thief. He is still a thief."

"Okay, Basit enough with this old nonsense, come and help me about my problem."

"You only have one solution, and it is Dambast[1] pray, and Sofi Abbas is master in that."

"Sofi Abbas is dumb, how can he write this pray for us?"

"You leave it to me, let's go!"

"It's evening."

"So what? Let's go."

It was a cloudy evening, but it wasn't raining. They went towards the house of Sofi Abbas. It wasn't so far.

"I heard a wolf Dambast, but this is a new one," Haji Baxtyar said.

Haji Basit couldn't hear him and he only shouted, "I can't hear you. What did you say?"

"I advised you to see a doctor to flush your ears!"

"A little louder, I can't hear you."

"I said, I heard of the wolf Dambast prayer, but I didn't know anything about rain Dambast!"

"If you continue to these kinds of marriage, you will need Dambasts, even for snakes and ants."

"Don't make a joke of it. I really didn't hear any of it!"

"People say he wrote a fire Dambast prayer for Hama Rashid Khan[2]."

Sofi Abbas was an old man who made a living by writing prayers and magic, he barely came out of his house, and nobody knows his family well. They say he was Khan's servant. Chief Salim said he is a good man.

---

[1] Kind of magic prayer that have been written on a paper to achieve some goals or intimidate a person

[2] One of the generals of Qazi Mohammad, and commander of Bana and suburbs.

Sofi Abbas welcomed them and Haji Basit explained the whole story to him. Sofi Abbas was silent. Under his white eyebrows that covered his eyes, he took a look at Haji Basit, then he closed his eyes. After a while, he brought a white paper and tore it into three smaller pieces and wrote something on each piece of paper, then he gave them to Haji Baxtyar, and turned to Haji Basit and said,

"Throw one of the papers in the river, the second one in the mosque pool and put the third one in Haji Baxtyar's pocket."

Haji Basit thanked him and gave him some money; then they left.

Araaz was so happy about the rain.

"I wish this rain will continue until winter because of the raining."

Daya Halaw, Miss Zinat and their friends would usually stay home during that time. Every day, Haji Baxtyar would visiting Daya Halaw. He completed the prayer jobs, the day after his meeting with Sofi Abbas. The ceremony field was a little below the Van tree. It was all muddy. Haji had a plan to make a bridal hut to protect them from the rain. For this, he had penetrated four long, sharp sticks in the four corners of the field and he wanted to cover its roof with nylon.

"The water level of the river has risen lately, Haji, put the sticks a little further."

"Don't worry, the rain will be finished soon!"

"The wedding arrived; the chef came by. Araaz woke up by the sound of drum and doorbell."

"Oh, my poor mum has no chance at all. First my dad, who she lost forever, and now this crazy man!" Araaz got angry at these all noise.

For the first time after leaving Halabja, Daya Halaw did some make up, and applied red henna on her hair; Miss Zinat did Daya Halaw's hair."

"Miss Zinat, are you sure it won't burn my skin until tomorrow?" Daya Halaw asked.

"You are absolutely right, but this henna is a good stuff, not to worry at all."

Araaz was still in bed when his mum screamed for help.

"Fariba, help me, my head skin is burnt completely. I told Miss Zinat, she didn't listen to me," Daya Halaw cried out, calling Fariba.

Fariba went to help Daya Halaw.

"Oh, your skin is burnt, we have to wash it with cold water."

Meanwhile, somebody knocked on the door. Araaz opened the door. It was the chef and his two pupils; they came in and Haji Baxtyar also entered after them.

"Why didn't you show up earlier? It is late!" Haji asked.

"Nobody has woken up yet?" Araaz grumbled.

"According to the Israel radio station news, today is also raining, but I am so happy, because all their prediction is a lie."

"So, why do you always listen to this radio station if you don't believe it? You also blame it for belonging to Jews, and being enemy of Islam; despite all these, you listen to its news most of the time."

"Oh my God, what happened to you, Daya Halaw?"

Daya Halaw didn't look at Miss Zinat and said, "Daya Halaw's head has been burnt by that good stuff henna!"

"You are absolutely right, God damn me!"

Daya Halaw asked her, to roll a cigarette.

Haji was only looking at the sky. He prepared the bridal hut. Haji Baxtyar's relative were there sitting on the chairs. The river level had risen, picking up more water from Sartoon Mountain and emptying it into the river. The guests were arriving gradually. Araaz put on a black Kurdish suit and Fariba wore green clothes and her ankle bracelet that were shining even under that weak sun. Dlir, who became friends with Ashmol, didn't leave Rozhan's arms even for a moment. The guest was gathered and the music was playing.

"Please call him again, Araaz!" Daya Halaw wanted Araaz to call his uncle Ibrahim.

"He is not answering, mum, he is busy."

"Send him a message. I want him, to know about my wedding."

"Mum, I told you, he is not answering at all, even if he answers, how could he come here in such rainy weather. Uncle Ibrahim is in Sullymani; if he moves now, he will be here in two days."

Haji Baxtyar and Daya Halaw greeted the guests and went towards their bridal hut. After lunch, the guests gathered to dance again.

While Haji was happy about Sofi Abbas's prayer, the clouds were roaring in the mountain. Away from the eyes of the guests, bride and groom, little by little the sun left the sky, and it started raining again. The first drop of the rain fell on the face of dance group. The young didn't care about the rain, and they were dancing eagerly.

"I said, why don't you roll one cigarette from that green tobacco, Halaw?" Haji Baxtyar asked.

"Don't worry, I already did," Daya Halaw answered.

Chief Salim shouted, "We have to stop and leave here, it is dangerous." But Haji Baxtyar didn't hear him at all.

Hama, who was playing drum on the top of the Van tree abruptly shouted, "Flood!"

But nobody heard him too. Haji Baxtyar and Daya Halaw were over the moon, they were laughing and giggling. Haji put his hand on Daya Halaw's leg and rubbed her feet; there was no shyness feeling, and nobody was important for them …

Suddenly, everyone left the field and ran. Araaz and Haji's son wanted to save them, but it was too late. The flood, with an ultimate anger, caught them. Haji was lying on Daya Halaw and couldn't hear anything. The first strike of the flood took them away in a flash. The screams of the women and children, and the roar of the river was mixed along with the sound of thunder. Chief Salim and Imam Abeed were completely wet. They came to Araaz, who looked at his mum and Haji Baxtyar from the roof. They had been swept away by the anger of the river.

"Sofi Abbas, did you pray for stopping the rain, or for calling the flood …?" Nobody heard Haji Baxtyar's last scream.

"We can't do anything for them until it stops raining."

Araaz got crazy. He came down and along with Haji's son, ran after the flood.

The flood ruined the wedding and destroyed all signs of happiness. The villagers waited until the rain stopped. After that they crossed the bridge and went to their houses.

Araaz and Haji's son were searching everywhere for them, but there was no sign of them. Araaz was exhausted, he couldn't walk anymore.

Until now, he could hardly endure the loss of his father, but from now, on he didn't know how to get along with this grief, a terrible grief. He was almost certain, that they would not survive this flood.

"Let's go, we cannot do anything!"

Chief Salim called out the inhabitants of the villages down the river to search for any trace of them. Some villagers also searched the beach by tractor; it rained continuously for three days.

Through the window, Araaz was looking at the river, he was so angry because he knew that he couldn't resist against unkind life, because his present and his future was not in his hand. Complain was meaningless for him. To whom could he complain? Although his heart was full of complain about the life, destiny, immigration, and the scream that nobody heard that. In one moment, his city, his house, friends and all his memories got lost. After Saddam Hussein's fall, they had built all their hope on Kurdish government.

But the end of most dreams, in this land, are tragedy. The only difference between Saddam's Halabja and Kurdish Halabja was diversity in the types of its demolition. Kurdish demolition was a modern one. In a moment, his mother was swept away by the flood!

Araaz was walking in the streets, searching all the houses. He looked at the trees and listened to the voices of the birds.

Hey mum, look! It is our Fig tree and this is Mr. Homar's house. Mum, here streets still live in the illusion of old Halabja, the trees still smell the breath of suffocated children of old Halabja. When will the shadow of death leave this city? They went to Kamaran's house, his uncle's son.

After the chemical bombing, all the survivor became refugee somewhere. They also stayed in Sullymani until the Islamic revolution of Iran. God bless Kak Ibrahim. He helped them much.

Kamaran lost his two daughters in the bombardment, only his son, Peshraw, who was breast-fed at that time, survived.

"What happened to our house, Kamaran?"

"I tried hard, but your house had been occupied by a Kurdish official due to its precious location. When I told them that this house is yours, they answered, 'we don't know anybody by that name'."

Kamaran stood up. He brought a bag and opened it for us.

"I took these staff from one of your neighbours." There was a picture of Araaz's family. Araaz was wearing one shoe in the picture, he was crying, but the voice of Ahmad and Halaw (who were laughing) could be heard inside the frame.

"What are you laughing about? Are you laughing at me? At my cry! No, it is me, who cries about my destiny, my sad destiny. Ha ha! My crying in that picture is still continuing."

"Enough with the crying, Araaz, it has been three days that you have been staring at this picture and crying, Rozhan brought us Trkhina[1]."

Due to the operations of Kurdish parties, Iran closed the border, nothing entered Iran's border from Bashur. So, like others, Araaz practically became jobless. Most of the time, like an aimless crazy one, he walked by the river hoping to find a trace of his mother, until one day he found his mother's tobacco bags, the bigger bag was full, but the smaller one was almost empty, the last few days sun had dried them up. He

---

[1] Kurdish food

remembered the time his mother wanted him to bring her tobacco, "Araaz please bring me some of this green tobacco!"

And he replied her, "Why does only the green tobacco gets finished?"

"I have much pain, you don't know, how much my knee hurts?"

And he answered sarcastically, "Your knees or Miss. Zinat and Haji Baxtyar?

And she would defend them desperately.

During the few months in Iraqi refugee's camp, all of his mother's hair turned white. She was waiting for Araaz's dad. The waiting that lasted for about fifteen years. *My mum died, when she lost her hope to find her husband.*

People die when they lose their hope. There are so many dead in this land, who only play the role of the livings, on the stage of the life.

"People say, when hatred replaces love, the real death would happen," Fariba said.

"Love is part of human's hope. If love dies, hate takes its place and humans become worse than dead. When the soul is wounded there is no cure, this wound becomes deeper and wider.

"Hate is the only human's truth thar doesn't disappear even after death!"

"Here, Araaz, in our land, more than any places on the earth, death is close to the human," Fariba continued.

"What about hate?" asked Araaz.

"Poor baby, give me a hug!" Fariba hugged him.

"But for me, waiting for my parents is worse than death!"

10

Araaz woke up early in the morning. Like always, he kissed Fariba's mole and got up. Dlir was stuck to Fariba tightly. Araaz threw his blanket over them.

"If you come back early, buy a chicken," Fariba told him.

Araaz pulled the curtain aside and looked out from the window. The weather was clear and there was cloud in the sky.

"Do we need anything else?"

"No, nothing."

"Put on warm clothes, it is cold!"

Fariba took out her head from under the blanket and yawned.

"Where did you put the warm clothes?" asked Araaz.

"They are in that black bag."

Ashmol woke up and looked at Araaz. Araaz who knew her look, poured a pot of milk for her.

When he put on his dress, he felt that it was big for him. He took his car out of the yard. Two waiting eyes were looking from the upstairs window.

There were so many sparrows sitting on the branches of Van tree; their chirps were mixing with the ripple of the river. Some crows were just waking up on the willows by the river, a heavy fog covered Sartoon Mountain. Although there were a few days of summer left, October was slowly showing itself. The village elders heard from their fathers that after drought and famine of the black plague year, which killed half of the inhabitants, the other half went to the old cave and prayed for forty days. They didn't come out of the cave until it started raining. By God's will, it started raining such heavy rain that lasted for ten days, then a horrible flood washed all the region; it was in October.

"Don't forget to buy some bread, Araaz, we have run out of bread," Fariba called out through the window.

When he wanted to close the door, he saw a blue Saipa Van car in front of the abandoned house next to them. Araaz looked at the house and was surprised. All those broken windows were replaced by the new ones, and they had been painted green. They also had curtain.

"Araaz, Araaz."

"What? Why don't you sleep?"

"I heard a strange sound!"

"It is nothing, nothing, you were just dreaming."

"Dream what, it came from that abandoned house."

Araaz was thinking about what Fariba said last night, when a loud voice of a man startled him.

"Hello, I am Rahman Axay Ashpoka."

Same as Mr. Zinat had described, he wore a red Persian coat and a black Kurdish pants. His two front teeth were made of gold, and he combed his gray hair to right side of his face. It was clear that he had shaved his beard this morning. He shook Araaz's hand tightly.

"You're welcome, I am Araaz."

At the moment Araaz and Rahman axa were greeting each other, three women three women, through the wooden window that the smell of it's fresh paint was spread, were stacking them.

"I don't think, he would be married."

"See if he has a ring or not."

"Don't snoop around others life, it is none of your business."

"My father is blocking my view." The sparrows on the Mulberry tree also welcomed their new landlord by first poop on Rahman axa's red coat.

"Rahman axa, I am at your service, anything you need, just tell me," Araaz said and then left there to buy bread for Fariba. Before he arrived at the bakery, there had been a huge fight there. After a lot of argument, the bakery calmed down, but the murmuring still could be heard, he thought that the fight was about the line.

"The recent Isis[1] attack on Kobani had a great influence on our people, and we had such useless arguments frequently at our bakery."

"What does the war of Isis have to do with this bakery?"

"You have no idea how many people have joined Isis in this city. Look at that old man who is sitting in the shadow. His nephew has joined Isis recently. The bread maker Mr. Salar asked him how he can stand with these wild killers. The old man answered that he stands with Islam, then the bread maker answered, 'the people of Rozhawa[2] are also Muslim, at least they are Kurd'."

---

[1] Islamic state of Iraq and Syria

[2] West part of Kurdistan

"Old man: our brothers only fulfil God's order."

After these argument, Mr. Salar couldn't control himself and threw a stone at him that hit the old man's head and injured him. People separated them; the old man was cursing and Mr. Salar shouted very loud, 'a single strand of Sharvan girl[1] hair, worth to all Isis world'.

The sound of Azan was mixed with the shouts of the potato seller. The sun was not as intense as before, a piece of pale cloud attached to the peak of Arbaba Mountain. They say that the dust will start again from tomorrow.

"I heard that you have got a new neighbour." It was Chief Salim with a book in his hand. He looked at Araaz under his sunglasses.

"Yes, we met this morning," answered Araaz.

"You want the same cigarette?"

"Yes please, and a half kilo of sunflowers seed."

"Mr. Araaz, try not to get too close to them, nobody knows them well. Every few years, one of them shows up. They all look alike; this year is a little bit different. They were here this morning, Rahman axa and his young daughter. He said that his daughter became a teacher, and only because of her, they came back."

On the top of the bridge, he saw a Gypsy Tent under the Van tree.

"Come on in, Mr. Araaz," Rahman axa greeted him.

"Let me take these stuff inside. I will join you then," Araaz answered him.

Araaz hugged and lifted Dlir up, then he went out to Rahman axa's tent.

---

[1] A fighter in Rozhawa, who fights against Isis is called Sharwan.

The squirrel was jumping up and down, on the top of the tree.

That poor baby was scared too much, lately the people hunted them ruthlessly. They say that, they make good money of selling squirrel, in Tehran. Rahman axa was sitting on a green plastic chair, taking off his red coat and wearing a short-sleeved colourful dress. He put his cell-phone in his pocket. He had tattooed his hand and all of his body. [A black snake that swallowed its tail, an English inscription, a bloody dagger] Rahman axa had already made a fire when Araaz arrived. When he saw Araaz, he stood up to greet him. He hugged Dlir and gave him a chocolate. Dlir got scared when he saw Rahman axa's gold teeth and burst into crying. Rahman axa grabbed a chair for Araaz quickly and said, "The tea will be ready soon."

Araaz looked around the tent, but unintentionally his eyes fell on the Rahman axa's tattoos again. He felt that he had seen one of them somewhere. That dagger …! He took out a cigarette and Rahman axa lit it for him by the fire. Araaz put his cigarette pack back in his pocket.

"It is Winston, yes?" Rahman axa asked.

"Oh sorry!" Araaz said, and gave him one of his cigarettes.

"It is red one, yes," said Rahman axa.

"Is that a good stuff?"

"No, there is nothing good in this country. People say it is made in Sullymani."

Rahman axa lit the cigarette and breathed in gently.

"I don't smoke these cigarettes, I smoke tobacco," Araaz said and he thought again about that dagger …

Oh! Now I remember, the first day, oh my God, that bloody dagger on that wall crack ...that's it.

Rahman axa noticed that Araaz was looking at his tattoos and said, "Each of these tattoos has its own story behind it, and I did each of them in a different place."

This image passed through Araaz's eyes, like a misty dream; the Van tree and its shadow, which, one day, was a hangout for revival of the dead laughter of his mother and the other villagers' women, that abandoned house next to them, which was more like a magic, the fury of the sky and rumblings of the flood ...now turned into a calm, blue sky, with a shining sun, stranger to the rain. And a fugitive man from the vortex of history took the places of his mum and those women's laughter. The abandoned house had also escaped from the magic of history, and it was populated again.

"Welcome, sir," a woman greeted Araaz.

Araaz raised his head. His eyes fell on a tall, blue-eyed blonde woman, who wore a blue dress. Neither the mum, nor the child wore a head scarf.

She had placed some glasses and a sugar cane on a steel tray.

"My wife, Zara," Rahman axa introduced her.

Araaz stood up to show respect, greeted her and introduced himself. She was a little bit old, but looked younger than Rahman axa. Miss Zinat would say that before Zara, he had married several times, but all his wives died as result of his bad behaviour.

A strange fear clutched Araaz's whole body, and when the cold and soulless look of Miss Zara met with the loud laughter of Rahman axa, his fear raised. Many people, without knowing them, aroused a pleasant feeling in you; they can

103

convey a warm feeling to you with a smile or a small laugh, but some people, as Miss Zinat said, are not friendly at all and you cannot feel good around them, even they might arouse the feeling of fear and hatred inside you.

"Come here, my daughters. Mr. Araaz and his kid are our honourable guest. What is his name?" Rahman axa pointed to Dlir.

"Dlir, his name is Dlir," Araaz answered.

Shawjwan and Awenya greeted Araaz and sat beside their mum.

Shawjwan was his eldest daughter, and like her mother she was blonde, but unlike her she had a fat face. She was wearing blue pants and white blouse. Although all her buttons were closed, her breast were still visible slightly. The day they arrived there, Araaz noticed that she limped a little. Later, she explained to Rozhan that, when she was in university, one day she had a date with her boyfriend in a park and the police were after them. They escaped from police and police took a shot at them and a bullet hit her leg. She hid it from her family and pretended that she fell down the stairs. Awenya was tall. She had black hair tied in ponytail style. She was wearing a short-sleeved red dress with a black skirt; her white legs and ankle bracelet were visible.

Two small black eyes, that their brightness was noticeable along with a mole on her neck made her beautiful a hundred-fold.

The flood left the town, but a big storm was about to happen. Miss Zinat said, whenever these gypsies come here, a great disaster would happen. Now these two lovebirds made things worse.

"May God have mercy on us."

Awenya took the tea tray for them. For a moment the, gloomy face of Araaz was drowned in the magical eyes of Awenya. This look swept through him and took him away to her magical world. A silvery voice, like the chirping of a strange morning bird, "Here you are, Mr. Araaz."

Rahman axa was singing an old Kurdish song, while he was making fire.

"Mr. Araaz, what happened? You look sad," Rahman axa started conversation.

Araaz explained the incident of flood and death of his mother for Rahman axa's family.

Rahman axa took out a small barbecue and put some charcoal on it and said,

"Araaz, you go inside, I have some work to do. I'm coming back in a minute."

There were some old-fashioned mats inside the tent. Strong smell like urine along with fire-smoke filled the entire tent. Rahman axa took out a brown Bafuri[1] from a black bag and cleaned its holes with a needle. He took out another small black bag from under the mats. It was opium. Araaz had smoked opium two times: once when he was in university and the other in prison, but not with Bafuri. They smoked opium until late at night. After that night, Rahman axa's tent became Araaz's second home.

Because of the closure of Iran-Iraq border, business had been decreasing and practically Araaz became jobless. Every day after lunch Araaz would go to Rahman axa's tent and they would spending their time together. After some days, son of Miss Zinat, Keywan, joined them too.

---

[1] An instrument for smoking opium

It was autumn, but there was no rain. "This year, we had no rain except for that, who came and swept away my mother," Araaz was complaining. Rahman axa was narrating his stories for them. Story of his journey to Afghanistan and his marriage.

"When I was in Kabul, I worked for a carpet seller, named Saied Golab. He was so experienced in antic and old staff. He had a white Russian Gas truck and he travelled to all parts of Afghanistan, searching for antic and old carpet and mat. We travelled together. I was young, ambitious and so curious to find new things.

"One day, we stopped for lunch in a village near Pakistan border, named Borabora. When my boss, Saied, wanted to do his prayer, the owner of restaurant guided him to a room in the back of the restaurant. After he completed his prayer and came out the room, he whispered in my ear, 'there is an old precious carpet in that room that has been dated back to more than five hundred years'. An old woman and a ten to twelve-year-old kid were the owner of the restaurant.

"After the launch, Saied went to the old woman and presented her a bottle of perfume to start a conversation, and then he brought up the topic of the carpet. The old woman was thrilled by his present and answered, 'there were two of these carpet. My father gave each of them to me and my sister for our wedding gifts. My sister got married before me, and she travelled to a village, on the other side of the border. After a few years, she died of cancer. I don't know what happened to the carpet then. If you can find that and bring it to me, I'll give you both for free'.

"Saied looked at me and lit a cigarette. During that era, there was severe war between former Soviet Union and the radical Islamic groups, and we knew how dangerous it was to cross the border.

"Saied got into the car and said, 'If we can find both carpets, we will live like a king for the rest of our life'. We decided to leave after the night prayer. Saied took his pistol and some bullets and hid it under his shirt. The ride was only an hour, but since we didn't know the area, we were on the road for around six hours. When we reached the village, it was Morning Prayer time. After prayer, we stayed in the mosque for a while, until the weather became clear. Rahman, Rahman". It was said, who called me. I was about to fall asleep when he said, 'we don't search for the carpet anymore'. It was like I was dreaming, because Saied never leaves such a treasure behind. I asked, 'do you want to quit?' He answered. 'Quit what? Are you crazy? Look at the carpet you slept on.' I looked at the carpet with surprise, then I looked at Saied again. What I was sitting on was a precious treasure that everyone dreamt about. He put his hand under the carpet and rubbed it on his face. One by two metres. 'How can we take it?' asked Saied.

"It was crowded inside the mosque and some armed men were standing outside. We decided to take it away at night. That village was being controlled by Islamic groups. We came out to have breakfast at a café near the mosque. Saied initiated conversation with the owner of Café. He told him that we came from Islamabad. On the outskirts of the village there was a fresh spring water. We went there to take a rest. We were about to fall asleep when suddenly, a loud voice woke us up. A man and a woman were shouting from a far distance, asking for help. They approached us; an old man and a young girl who wore a mask were running towards us. The old man shouted and escaped into the forest, but at the very moment, I saw with my own eyes the strangest thing in my life, that girl flew like a bird into the sky then disappeared. Saied and I were staring at the sky for a while, when the sound of gunfire brought us back to our sense.

"A couple of men were coming towards us. Three armed men got to us and asked, 'who are you? What are you doing here?' One of them, who had a long beard, fired a shot near our feet to intimidate us. It was more like a dream. Saied went forward to flatter them and after praying for Islamic fighters, explained that, 'we live in Islamabad, here is my ancestor's village my son like to visit here'. They asked us if we saw anybody nearby! Saied answered quickly, 'no, no we only heard some gunshots'. After some other questions, they freed us and left. That was the first time I saw death so close me. Said stared at the sky, but I looked at the person whom had been killed a moment ago and a woman that was crying on his corpse. We wanted to check if she was the same girl who flew like a bird! …but none of us dared to approach her, that's why we left by soon and returned to the café."

Keywan's phone rang. He went out of the tent and answered it quietly, Rahman axa prepared the Bafuri.

"Did you see the armed men again?"

"When we arrived the café, they were sitting there. Saied paid their bill and started to tell his stories. We said the night prayer with the people in the mosque. After that, one of the armed men invited us for dinner, but Saied thanked him and rejected his invitation. We waited until eleven at night, and after every one left the mosque, Saied went out and stood in the mosque exit door. Beside his pistol, he also had got a sharp knife. I went for the carpet. When I wanted to fold it up, I saw a paper stuck to the back of the carpet. It was like a map. I put the paper in my pocket and bent down to pick up the carpet. I was about to come down the stairs, suddenly the mosque servant blocked my way. He wanted to scream for help but Saied stabbed him in the neck from behind; his blood splashed on my face. I was scared too much; it was a dark night. We ran out of the mosque, but I felt that one car was chasing us. I saw its lights behind us.

'Don't worry, we are close; they cannot chase us after the border. When we crossed the border, they'll stop chasing us.'

The car got closer and we ran into the jungle. Because of the mountainous area and the darkness, we couldn't run fast.

'We are almost there,' said Saied, and he throw the carpet upward with happiness, 'we are almost there.'

"We got so excited over reaching the border, that we forgot the car that was chasing us. I heard some shotguns. Unfortunately, a bullet hit Saied's head. I only remember that Saied hugged the carpet while he fell down from a high cliff. I escaped from them, but after a while, I felt a bad pain in my belly. I was bleeding and I fell on the ground. The blood was coming from my feet. I held my belly and laid down. I was staring at the sky. The white thing was moving among the stars. It came down and down. A winged woman, whose white hair was spread on her wings approached me. I thought she was death angel. When she got closer, I felt that I knew her somehow. Yes, it was her, the same woman who flew to the sky and disappeared!

"When I regained my consciousness, I was lying on a blanket in a small room. The sunlight entered the room through the window hole and was right on my head. There was a cooper tray on the shelf, laden with a glass and a water pot. I wanted to stand up, a disembodied voice from the other side of the door told me 'Don't move' she came in to my bedroom. I was surprised; she was the owner of café. The old woman who has sent us after the carpet.

"You wanted to kill us? I asked.

'Silence, I didn't send you; you went after your greed. God had mercy on you, our people were there and saved you. My daughter told me you're almost dead.

"We were in the middle of our conversation when her daughter entered the room. I was confused. I wasn't sure if whether I was hallucinating or crazy. The angel whom I saw was the same girl that flew into the sky and disappeared. The same girl who saved my life. A tall angel with black eyes. She came closer and looked at my wound, her breasts smelled like lemon. I felt hot and dizzy, then I passed out again.

"One night, during the nights that I was recovering, she came to my room again. I only recognized her by her scent. I got better by her sound of her breathing. She was doing a tattoo on my hand and arm, slowly and secretly.

"Except for the dagger, all these tattoos are her work. After a while, I could stand on my feet, but I haven't seen her again; it was like she had returned to the sky, I don't know…, it was more like a sweet dream. When I asked the old woman about her daughter, she smiled and answered, 'I have only one daughter who found you that night, wounded and then saved you'. I wanted to show her my tattoos, but I changed my mind. I found the old map in my bloody clothes."

Rahman Axa stood up and a brought out a yellowish paper out of his notebook. It was a folded map on which a few dried drops of blood could be seen. Keywan came closer and Rahman Axa put on his glasses and opened the map widely.

"When I returned to Kabul, I went directly to our shop. Since Saied Golab had no family there, I became the owner of his shop. The job was great, I had many customers and visitors including Russian customers who visit my shop a lot. One day, I was alone and I didn't have any work to do, so I opened the map. I didn't know much about old maps. When I was trying to find a clue on the map, somebody opened the door. He was one of the Russian guys. He came inside. He was an old man around the age of 60; he could speak Persian very well. He had been living in Afghanistan since The Soviet Union invasion. He saw the map and grabbed it and then sat down. He looked at it for a minute, then he asked me, 'where did you get this map?'. I described my story to him. He looked closer at the map. This time he wrote some Russian words on a paper, then he explained, 'this map marked the location of an old treasure from the time of Alexander the Great, which is located in the west Iran between two rivers'.

"After I returned to Kurdistan, I have tried to find it several times, but I couldn't. This year, I hope to find it anyway possible, and for this job, I need some experienced and reliable friends."

Keywan and Araaz looked at each other, then they looked again at Rahman Axa who was smoking his Bafuri. "These few days that I have met you, I know that I can trust you. I'm an experienced man. I have travelled to many countries. I have lived amongst many different people, that's why I am a wise man, and I'm sure that I can trust you for this mission."

Araaz and Keywan promised Rahman Axa to keep that secret to their graves. "We can't dig that place, unless a considerable rain softens the soil. We have to wait for the rain." Rahman axa hadn't told them the exact location of the treasure.

"Brothers kill each other for treasure." With this quote, Rahman axaa finished his story.

11

It was autumn and schools were opened. Rahman axa's younger girl, Awenya, was an English teacher. She woke up early in the morning, before Araaz and Fariba, and put on pink lipstick, covered her hair with scarf and wore a long dress. The school was close to her house, on the other side of the river, two allies after the clinic!

At the beginning, her father used to take her to school, but when she learnt how to get there, she went by herself. When she was going to school, Keywan had gone to Kolbari much earlier, her father also had collected fire wood in the back field and it had been a long time since Imam Abeed called the Azan.

The beauty of Awenya became famous among the teachers and the villagers. Her manners made her more beautiful. There was a rumour that she had a fiancé, but she wasn't showing it. From the very beginning, one of the teachers named Hazhar, who was a tall and handsome guy, fell in love with her.

The rain and flood of August predicted a rainy year, but it was autumn and there was no sign of rain yet. The fields were thirsty and drought. Elders of the village and Imam of the mosque prayed to God, asking for rain several times, but to no avail. The villagers who got disappointed about the rain prayer that they turned to Booka Barana[1], an old Kurdish tradition. Booka Barana was an old custom of Kurdistan in the time of drought and hunger. It was a symbol for the Goddess of water. The villagers showed the thirst of the Earth to their God by colourful clothes and reciting poems, hoping to satisfy the Goddess of water. In every region, they make Booka Barana in different shapes. The history of this tradition is as old as Kurdistan, but people of this village and the villages around had a bad memory about Booka Barana's tradition. Last time in the spring after the Islamic Revolution of Iran, there was a big drought in Rozhalat and because of that drought all those villages made their own Buka Barana and headed towards the lovers' graves. The girls on their way were reciting the poem of Buka Barana. During that time, Islamic Regime declared war against Kurdistan. First, the regime bombarded towns and villages with helicopters and war planes without considering the civilians. On that day, Kurdish ceremony, all the girls were singing Buka Barana wants water, she wants water for the farms.

What else does poor have Kurdistan besides landscapes and mountains?

Kurdish cities were under the control of Kurdish parties. Each party had their own armed troops. Islamic regime was bombarding any of kind of meetings, unfortunately they considered The Buka Barana ceremony as a political meeting, and bombed them. That Buka Barana didn't ask for bombs and rockets, she didn't want blood, but the streams were filled

---

[1] Kurdish old tradition, included making a painted doll and singing ask for rain

with the blood of Buka Barana girls, springs were reborn with reborn, and Buka Barana also made her lipsticks by the blood of those martyr girls. The red colour. All the martyrs were buried below the lovers' graves and they laid the Buka Baranas on their graves.

Nowadays even after many years, their clothes are still fresh and their lips are still red. Two days later, on a sad dark night when the people of the village were asleep, the sound of rain woke them up Miss Zinat who was still waiting for the rain, got excited and came out. She wanted to see the first rain. She promised herself to take a shower under the rain. She shouted, "It's raining, wake up people, it's raining." But after a couple of minutes, she smelled a strange scent. Blood was dropping down from her head and face. The streams were filled with blood, the springs were reborn with blood.

The villagers didn't come out until the end of the month. They thought Doomsday was upon them. Wise men of the village believed that it was the wrath of the Goddess of water, and the magic of the Buka Barana. All the people were praying to God hoping for forgiveness, until one morning the sun showed up and put an end to this magic. Miss Zinat would say that during the moonlight nights of that year, the Buka Baranas were flying in the sky. Until the end of Iran-Iraq war, Buka Barana tradition was not held in those villages, due to the bad memory of the villagers, but in a sad, dried autumn, people turned to the Buka Barana again. This time, something even stranger happened. Some people attacked the ceremony and injured some of the villagers. They attacked people by the slogan of La Illaha Illallah[1]. They believed that this tradition

---

[1] Islamic slogan

115

was against Islam, and it was idol worship and they should pray only to God (Allah). They were some filthy men that covered their faces with a mask. After their attacks, they went to the graveyards and broke tombstones and tore apart the clothes of the Buka Baranas with their swords, but the lips of the Buka Baranas were still red and fresh. That night, some other villagers also saw the Buka Baranas in the sky. After that, nobody dared to make a Buka Barana. Buka Barana and its tradition was replaced by praying to God in Arabic, asking for rain. Afterwards, there were no signs of the women, coloured clothes, poems or songs. There were only some grumpy men and the Imam of the mosque who were praying to God asking for rain.

The principal of the school gathered the teachers and told them to help the students. The parents were also helping their children to learn the poem of the ceremony. On Friday, the villagers in company with the other villagers around headed towards the lovers' graves. Fariba, Rozhan, Shawjwan and Araaz attended the ceremony. Awenya and the other teachers also participated. The Imam and some elders of the village believed that this tradition is satanic and against Islam. On Friday's prayer, the Imam said, "It's satanic ceremony and their parents must not allow their children attend this ceremony," but most of the people attended the ceremony. Chief Salim also participated in recited the poem with the others. It was the moment of truth for Hama to play his drum. He was circling among the women and played the drum for them. For the first time, Hazhar shared his feelings with Awenya, "I want to tell you that I love you," He revealed his secret and opened his heart for Awenya. Awenya did not answer his love proposal directly, but it was obvious that she was hiding something, a secret.

A few months later, he remembered the first date of Hazhar and Awenya at the Buka Barana ceremony, when Araaz was standing in front of Rahman axa's house, and a tall handsome guy was crying. "You betrayed me, you ruined my life, you are a killer."

Some nights, after they took Buka Baranas to the lover's graves, the villagers were coming out looking at the sky, searching for Buka Barana, but no one saw it. The first drop of rain fell on Keywan's forehead, who came to open his mother's door. It started to rained and it continued for twelve days. Rahman axa packed his tent. He rarely came out of the house, except for taking his daughter to school. "It has been two years that you've only stared at this map. You searched every place this treasure, but—"

"Quiet, I found it here," Rahman axa didn't let her wife finish her words. As soon as the rain stopped, he spread his tent again. On an evening, he called Araaz and Keywan, asking them to be ready mission. "It is time! You have to be ready for tomorrow. We will go in the evening." Rahman axa determined the time and he warned them again to keep the secret. The next day, in the afternoon, they put the shovel and the pickaxe and all the necessary equipment in Rahman axa's car and then left. They were on their way for two hours, a winding and spiral road. Little by little, darkness covered the sky. The headlights of the car were not illuminating the road and the dust was mixed with darkness.

The sound of Rahman axa's car was the only thing that was attacking the darkness. Rahman axa reduced his speed and stuck his head out of the car and said, "We have almost arrive, we have to cross the river." He stopped the car on the other side of the river and they took the things out of the car quickly.

Rahman axa made a small tent and put the things inside it. He took out a strange device among their stuff, turned it on and checked the device by dragging it slowly on the ground.

"Is it a gold detector?" asked Araaz.

"Yes, it is," answered Rahman axa, and he was checking the ground everywhere around. After a while, the metal detector started to make a noise in the lower part of the spring. Rahman axa ignored the sounds and went back to the upper part of the spring, then he returned to the spot of the sound. The device started beeping again, Araaz ran towards Keywan and shouted,

"Hurry up, let's go, we found it."

"We have to dig this place," said Rahman axa.

Keywan and Araaz started to dig the ground by pickaxe, they dUg the ground, and Rahman axa threw away the dirt and soil by shovel. They placed a lamp on a stone to brighten the hole. From time to time, Rahman axa took off his map and glanced at it, then he put it back to his pocket.

During two hours, they dug two metres, but there was no sign of any treasure.

"Are you sure this is the right spot?" asked Keywan. He got exhausted and went to the spring and brought some water. Except for the howling of wolves, not a sound was to be heard.

"Come on, we have to find it tonight!" Rahman axa said.

At that moment, Rahman axa didn't seem old at all; he was digging the ground like a twenty-year-old guy. Their clothes were covered in sweat and mud, completely.

It was around one past mid-night, and they still had found nothing.

Keywan suggested to check the metal detector again. He got very tired and laid on his back and stared at the sky. Rahman axa and Araaz were digging the ground without stop.

"Araaz, Araaz, Rahman axa," Keywan pointed to the sky and shouted.

The pick fell out of Araaz's hands.

A woman came out of nowhere and sat near the spring in the dark. Araaz got very scared. Rahman axa saw the scene and stopped digging, then with no hesitation, he went towards the spring. When he got there, he asked,

"What happened? You show up again!"

The white woman looked at Rahman axa for a moment, then she flew to the depth of the sky.

"Let's hurry up, we are so close to our treasure."

Araaz believed that it was only a white, big bird, and nothing to be scared about, but Keywan, who saw the girl, clearly turned pale with fear. He got scared more than anything else before in his life. That fear was more horrible than going to jail, worse than execution.

He had never been scared more.

It was past three mid-night, the place they were digging was now a huge and wide hole. They were completely exhausted, when suddenly, Keywan called Rahman axa, "Come down here and bring the lamp." Two stone-slabs were appeared under the dirt. Rahman axa went down and wiped the mud with his hand, then he lifted one of the stone.

"It is a grave!" said Rahman axa.

Keywan held the lamp for him, while Araaz was guarding the hole. There was a small mummy inside the grave, and there were pictures of a snake and a dagger carved on the other stone-slab.

They took off the mummy quickly and wrapped it up with some clothes. Rahman axa put it in the car. Araaz looked back at the grave to make sure there was nothing left. He went down inside the hole. He noticed that a necklace was left there, a strange necklace that had four pink amber stones and two teeth. Araaz took a short look at the necklace and put it in his pocket fast, then he came up the hole and joined them quickly. They packed immediately and headed back towards the village.

"I called him several times, the customer is on his way to see the mummy. Not to worry," Rahman axa answered Keywan who was asking a lot. Araaz got off his car and entered the tent, while Rahman axa was watching an Arabic sexy dancer on his phone.

Rahman axa's endless sexual desire was not hidden to anybody.

"That rude bastard is like an old wolf, he never takes of his eyes from me," said Miss Zinat. "He stares right at my breasts."

Rahman axa became the most discussable topic for the women of the village, lately. One day, Rahman axa described a memory about how when he was young, he had been captured by Greek police, because he raped a Greek woman in public. Rahman axa's life was full of these kinds of stories. Keywan believed that most of his stories were lies, but Araaz believed that this man was mentally sick.

A few days later, in a morning on December, when Araaz was warming up his car, Rahman axa came to him and after greeting, he told Araaz that the customer will arrive today and he wanted Araaz not to leave village. Araaz had to return home. He drove the car to the yard and turned it off, and after a long discussion with Fariba, left the house and went to Rahman axa's tent.

"Keywan is not answering my call!" complained Rahman axa.

"He must have gone to the border," Araaz answered him and asked, "when will he arrive?"

"He said that he'll call me when he gets there. We have to go to bring him here."

Rahman axa went out to collect wood, while Araaz was making tea.

At that moment, Rahman axa's phone rang. Rahman axa answered his phone and when he finished, he pointed to Araaz.

"Let's go, he's arrived in the city."

They took Araaz's car. The customer gave them a hint to follow him. He was a short, bald man who has worn sunglasses. They sat inside the tent, and started talking with Rahman axa, while Araaz was making tea. The customer was Turkish, but he had lived in Tehran for many years, and Rahman Axa said that, he had a big antique shop at the Manoochehri Street in Tehran. Rahman axa wanted him to stay for a while and rest, but he was in a hurry and he wanted to see the mummy first, so Rahman axa, without any delay, stood up and went to bring the mummy.

When the customer saw the mummy, he couldn't control his feelings.

He took off his sunglasses and put on another one to have a closer look at the mummy. He came closer and asked, "Wasn't there anything else with the mummy?"

'Like what?" asked Rahman axa.

"Like a document or anything to prove its authenticity."

Rahman axa put down the cup and remembered.

"There was a picture of a snake and a dagger on the stone."

The man asked us to bring that stone too, because it is an identity document for the mummy.

"Where did you find this? Through a map or …?"

Rahman axa didn't let him finish, and brought the map.

The sound of a car was coming from outside.

"Don't worry, it is Keywan," Araaz assured them and poured another tea for them, and asked Keywan where had been.

"We called you several times."

"Where? I have only two places, either Kolbari or hospital. I took my wife to the hospital," Keywan answered.

"Why didn't you answer our calls?"

He took off his phone and said, "It fell and broke yesterday."

That day, the customer left and told them to bring that stone.

Next day, they found the stone in the grave. They put the stone in the car quickly, and came back to the tent.

That night, Araaz showed the necklace to Fariba and explained everything to her.

"Why didn't you tell me these things? Why did you hide it?"

Araaz put the necklace on Fariba's neck for a moment and told her that, this necklace was also in the grave.

"Araaz, I don't trust that man."

12

The weather was so cold that some nights, the river would freeze. The snow was slowly covering the mountains, especially Sartoon Mountain peak was completely blanketed with snow, but it was snow flurry in the farms.

Awenya hooked up with Hajar, since the day of Bouka Barana ceremony.

Hajar raised this issue with his family. Although his father was against this relationship, but since Hajar was the only child of his parents, nobody would stand against him. Awenya's behaviour had completely changed. She wasn't happy any more. Shawjwan and her mother notice this change. They were well aware of Awenya and Hajar's relationship. Every night, Awenya would stay alone in her room and stare at her old gifts. She locked the door, and brought up her old photos and the other presents …She was crying on her photos, she was also hiding her ring, and she was talking on her phone until late at night …

"Until when you want to live like that?" Shawjwan mocked her. "Ha Ha! It was your fairy love story …you said that you would die for him."

Shawjwan and her mother's mockery made her angry. Awenya didn't know how to cope with Shawjwan's mockery.

Her hatred of Shawjwan got stronger, when she illustrated her satanic laughter and devilish deeds, she had done to separate them.

"You are pathetic," Shawjwan continued. He came for me and proposed to me before you, but what I have done. I refused to even answer him and ignored him totally."

Shawjwan was master at breaking Awenya down and making her angry.

"Ok, you and mum won, I quit, now are you happy, aren't you?" Awenya cried.

"Why should we be happy? You betrayed him yourself, you knew that he was far away, and as soon as a new rich guy came to you, you forgot everything immediately."

Awenya was crying. Shawjwan mockery now became torture. The only person, she could trust and share her feeling with, was her friend Snoor."

"Awenya, if Hawre finds out about this, how would you answer him? You are, all his hope …"

Hawre and Awenya knew each other through Facebook. Awenya was a student in Tabriz University.

One autumn morning Awenya did her makeup and went outside.

"Where do you want to go?" asked Snoor.

Awenya went on her first date with Hawre at Ilguli Park in Tabriz.

A tall boy, who had worn sunglasses and tied his hair, was waiting for her.

"Oh, Snoor, I wanted to talk with this boy for eternity." Hawre was working in Agriculture centre in Rasht.

Awenya visited him every month, and stayed with him for a couple of days. Their love affair from a puppy love, turned to a real one.

"Tell him to come to your family for the proposal," Snoor insisted because she knew that Hawre couldn't get along with Awenya's family, that's why, she wanted to put an end this useless relationship.

After one year, Hawre sent his family to Rahman axa's house. Hawre had been sure about the answer of Rahman axa, but he didn't know that Rahman axa's decision was not the final one. After a week, Awenya's family rejected their proposal. Shawjwan knew that they loved each other too much, and she was jealous about it, so she did everything in her power to separate them.

Once she called Hawre by a different phone numbers, and wanted him to regret his decision.

She didn't do this only for Hawre, Shawjwan did that with everyone that Awenya loved. She got really tired.

Until one night a big fight happened and Awenya ran away from the house. She didn't know where to go?

Coldness, tears and darkness, together with despair, was mixed with her doomed destiny.

Araaz was coming back home. He stopped the car and said,

"Miss Awenya …

13

No one can cross this blizzard."

"Don't worry, I have a wheel chain."

They also had wheel chain, but they got stuck on the way.

December welcomed the snow at the end of autumn.

"Death in the autumn is legendary."

"What about autumn death?"

"Autumn never dies!"

"Push it, we are almost there, a little more please."

"Don't step on the gas, shift the gear to number two."

"I wonder, if he arrived! He doesn't answer his phone."

"Do you have any cargo?"

"How much do you charge for carrying one TV to Tabriz?"

"The road, cold weather and waking up early in the morning!"

"That Oil heater smells awful, change the wick."

"I changed it recently, it is because of the fuel, open the door."

He left the TV seller's shop.

"Make me an omelette, sir."

Thick smoke was inside the Café.

"Bring Mr. Araaz a strong tea."

"Now, the heater is adjusted."

"Two eggs, Mr. Araaz?"

He dried his pants by the heater, steam and smoke were mixed.

"Make it three eggs, okay!"

Araaz took his cigarette pack out of his pocket "God damn you,

Rahman axa, you nearly finished my cigarette." There were only two cigarettes left in the pack. He took out one, smelled it and put it between his lips.

"Take the salt to that Ajam[1]."

He pointed to the old man who sat next to Araaz. He was eating slowly, but he was chewing the food loudly. The smell of sweat and socks, samovar steam and cigarette smoke were mixed with cruel laughter.

"What is the dollar price today?"

"Mr. Araaz which one? Onion or pepper or Parsley?"

"Buy me some apricot lavash!" said Fariba.

All the scents mixed together, the smell of the smoke was most dominant, it was like streams of odours were joined in this cafe and they became a river, river of odours.

"Onion, please."

The cafe assistant was trying to kill a roach.

"Close the door, it is cold."

Sarchnars café was like a small Kurdistan. Saggez, Boukan, Krmashan, Bijar… the hunger collected all Kurdistan in this city. They were coming early in the morning, in hopes to find one cargo including the TV and washing

---

[1] In kurdistan, the people who are not Kurdish are called Ajam.

machine etc. They were caring the cargo to other cities for a low fee.

"Bring me another bread."

"Open the door a little, the smoke is almost killing us."

"Take another bread to Mr. Araaz!"

Fighting for a loaf of bread, escaping from the bombardment, execution and chemical bombs. Escaping got tired itself, and it doesn't know for how long, it will be with this poor nation. Most of the time, running is harder than death.

"It is too spicy, you put too much pepper in it."

Araaz looked at the old man, who was in front of him, with a smile. He lit a cigarette and stared at the board with Kurdistan flag on it, the flag of homeless nation.

"Please open the door …"

"Shut the door …"

"How much Mr.…"

Flag red, white, sun, green.

Araaz stood up to go out. He touched his face for a moment, remembered his broken nose and took a deep breath.

"A country without a flag or a flag without a country, we are an advanced nation, better to say scout nation, because we made our flag before our country!"

Araaz remembered the first slap in Krmashan prison.

"You want to create independent Kurdistan."

He remembered the first punch that broke his nose, after the slap.

"I can't go only with one cargo. In the afternoon, find me another TV."

Business was sluggish, winter had begun and Kolbari got harder in the snow.

They said, "Yesterday, two Kolbars fell down from the mountain and they are still looking for their bodies."

Life continued but with difficulty. Snow covered the streets. The business was not good, and shopkeepers were complaining about the economic situation all the time. Rumours of general strikes were heard. Last time, because of the killing of a Kolbar, shopkeepers of border towns went on a strike and closed their shops for a week. He was a twenty-year-old boy.

"Mr. Araaz, tomorrow you can come and take the TVs."

His ears were freezing.

"I have to buy some apricot lavashes for Fariba."

A young twenty-year-old boy was struggling with nature, to fulfil his dreams. What dream? Where on earth fighting for a loaf of bread is considered as a dream?

This Bazaar starts with the death of Kolbar and also ends with his death. In the middle of this hellish deception, we and the customers remain. We sell and they buy the commodities that goes on through the path of death.

Araaz was walking on the café street, hoping to find the bookseller there.

"Whisky, cards …"

He reached the river and went towards the café, but the café was closed and there was no sign of bookseller. "He hasn't come yet, because of the snow." To buy some apricot lavashes, he crossed the bridge. On the other side of the river, he bought the apricot lavashes and a couple of the headache pills. On his way back home, Araaz saw a man who sold beets. "Come on, beet, sweet and delicious, come here, boiled beet." Araaz craved boiled beets.

"How much is a kilo?"

The beet seller looked at Araaz with a frown and answered him.

It was him, the bookseller.

"Oh, it is you, I was just looking for you, where are your books," asked Araaz.

The man started laughing, and answered, "Yes, it is me. The books wished to turn into beets. Nobody reads book, but every one eats beet. How much do you need?"

"Two kilos, you don't want to tell me what happened to you?"

"I got arrested because of some illegal books. I was in prison for a while and they confiscated all my books."

"Oh sorry, that's too bad."

"No, don't be sorry at all, now I feel better and I am very happy. I used to get sad all the time, because I thought no one reads books, but now all my customers and I care about is, whether the beets are sweet or not. I like this job more than my other job."

"Why did you have another job besides selling books?"

"So many other jobs."

He took his hat off his head and scratched the back of his head with four fingers, then he wiped the dust off his hat, and added some sugar to the beets.

"I was only six when I started my first job. We lived in an old house on the outskirts of the town that was full of roaches. My mum was complaining all the time about that.

"'I can't live here anymore.'

"My poor dad did whatever he could, included pouring insecticide and some other stuff, but they were useless, until one day, he returned home with a swatter.

130

"'If you kill twenty roaches a day, I'll pay you one Toman[1] per roach.' He told me that if I kill less than twenty, I get nothing.

"'If I kill more?'

"'The same, twenty Toman.'

"I began from that day. The first day, I only killed fifteen, but day after day, I became more skilful and I reached a hundred roaches a day. Since my father rewarded me only twenty Tomans, I only delivered twenty roaches and saved the rest for the other days. Pretty much, my first job was hunting roaches. One day, my father asked me, if I knew the number of the roaches, I had killed. I answered 'immediately, 'three thousand and eight hundred'.

"'Good job my son!'

"My great fear was that, if one day the roaches would finish, what should I do? Until one day my father wanted to go on a business trip.

"'When will you come back, dad?'

"'Count till three thousand and eight hundred, and I'll be back, son.'

"My father was gone and after a while, there was no sign of the roaches in the house. I counted till three thousand and eight hundred, more than a thousand time, but my dad didn't come back home."

Araaz was staring at a yellow-hand, worn swatter that had been tied to his cart. He remembered this scene from their first meeting.

"I was looking for a novel, I hoped I could find it here," Araaz said.

---

[1] Iran currency

"Oh novel, story and poem!"

"What? It seems that you don't like them."

"Actually, I hate them."

"Literature is heart of society."

"Ha ha! A brainless society does not need a heart! This is the biggest disease of Middle East. This region is full of poets and novelist, but it doesn't have a good philosopher."

"Poetry itself, is philosophy."

"Which philosophy? Admiring the female organs and description of spring and autumn, how is it similar to Heidegger's philosophy. Descartes said, 'I think, therefore, I am.' Foucault says, 'I am writing, so I am.' What should we say? We are dead, because we don't think. We are here to eat, sleep and have sex. This is the summary of our philosophy. Most of us are proud of not thinking."

Araaz looked at his face and said, "First, I liked Saddegh Hedayat[1], then Kafka and Marquez, and lately Llosa and Borges. You are so pessimist about literature. Novel and poetry could save society from any type of radicalism. High culture redeems the society. Literature is one of the pillars of culture."

"Mr. Araaz, we are a nation who was born dead. We haven't got more than ten famous Kurdish novelist. At the time Astyages and Khosraw Parviz[2] were busy with killing and slaughtering, the Greeks built the foundation of philosophy with the idea of Plato and Aristotle. Take a look at Germany. It passed through two world war and its land were completely destroyed, but Germany stood up on its feet,

---

[1] Famous contemporary Persian writer. His masterpiece is The *Blind Owl* [2] Two of old Kurdish and Iranian king

rose again, and turned to the first power of Europe. This is the power of philosophy. They have Marx, Hegel, Kant and Heidegger."

"That's true, but they also have Goethe, Gunter grass and Kafka."

"I am not against novel and poetry, I say people must think."

The weather was getting dark, and Araaz wanted to return home.

"Nice to see you again," he took the beets and gave him the money.

"Come again, I'll be happy to serve you," said the beet seller.

Araaz said goodbye to him and left. He was confused by the bestseller's words, 'we were born dead', philosophy and poetry, thoughts and dreams. One is complicated and the other is easy to understand.

Coldness and silence of the streets were hand in hand dancing for the darkness.

"What about the Flag in the café board? Its pale colours, and its dusty sun."

"Oh, Dr. Dlir …"

His name was Dr. Dlir …I never forgot that boy. In the university compass, a blond, thin guy came and greeted me.

"I am Dlir, they told me you want to talk to me."

He was a medical student, he also liked music and poetry. He was from Krmashan. Dlir participated in all Kurdish ceremony in the university. He played piano, read poetry and had good knowledge about the history of Kurdistan, that's why I wanted to meet him. After the first meeting, we gradually got closer and became good friends. Although

133

sometimes we argued about political issues, but we made up quickly. We were together for two years and those two years were the best years of my life. He knew that I was in a relationship, but he had not met Fariba yet, until one day, me and Fariba were walking in an alley near the university. We held each other hands. I was looking for a safe place to kiss and hug Fariba. While I was searching all the place around, suddenly a car stopped and a man shouted, "What is your relationship with this lady?"

My heart was about to stop beating. Fariba's hands became cold in my hand. I was afraid to look back. Fariba whispered in my ear, "My father and brothers will kill me." After a moment, I heard a familiar laughter.

"Oh my god, Dr. Dlir, it was you!!"

We laughed at that scene for a long time.

"What are you doing for your life, Doctor?"

"Brain surgery, what am I doing? Don't you see? I am painting."

"What do you draw?"

"Why do you ask? You will see, when it is over, be patient!"

I went forward to see what he drew. It was written on the top of his board, 'dreams of a dead land'. For the first time, I saw Dlir was drawing.

"At the legend of homeless flag, I looked at spring that, on the edge of vague horizon was walking towards the colourful lie of morning light."

I saw autumn,
With a golden cigarette between her lips
In front of the eyes of

Those four frightened pigeons in the cage
Regardless of all cries of the scared leaves,
Was executing the colours of the flag
Summer was also standing on the burnt crops of
motherland, and
Cleaning its eyes with the worn scarf of
Omari Xawar[1]
Suddenly strong wind started to dance at the winter party
And drowned the legend.

"Sky without Sun or river without water? It is better to say, the sun without the sky, and water without a river, they just like a flag without a land. Trust me, they are like bodies without souls." The weather was getting dark, and Araaz wanted to go back home. Dr. Dlir got out of the Araaz's car, and said goodbye to Araaz, and then left.

Araaz started the car and drove towards home. When he reached near the bridge, he saw a tall woman walking fast.

"What is this woman doing here at this time of night?"

He lowered the car window. It was Awenya, the younger daughter of Rahman axa.

"Is that you, Miss Awenya?" asked Araaz, "get in the car, I'll give you a ride home!"

"Hi, Mr. Araaz, I don't disturb you," answered Awenya.

"Come on, get in the car, it is too late!"

It was clear that she had cried a lot.

"What happened? What are you doing out?"

Her eyes filled with tears again.

---

[1] One of the famous victims of chemical bombardment of Halabja, that his child was killed in his arms.

"Nothing, I can't stay at that home anymore. I want to die," she cried.

"My sister, it is not the right way, let's go to our house tonight, tomorrow I will talk with your father."

Finally, Araaz convinced her to come to his house, in spite of her resistance.

14

He had woken up with a monster headache. He had a bad dream in which a big black fish in the middle of a sea, was pulling him down to the depth of the water. He wanted to release himself, but he couldn't, until the fish itself freed him. He tried to pull himself up, but he felt that half of his body was eaten. The black fish was laughing at him loudly.

While his whole body was drenched with sweat, he woke up and pulled aside the curtain to look outside. It wasn't morning yet. It was raining cats and dogs, heavier than yesterday. The morning rain for a heart-broken one is not like the other rain. It breeds hatred in the heart and ignites the flame of revenge. He took a headache pill and put it in his mouth, but he didn't swallow it. He wanted to feel the bitterness of the pill, then he sat on a chair, in front of the window, and stared at those three trees outside. He didn't remember the name of the tree. Indeed, at that situation, he was not conscious of so many things around him, neither the time, nor the place …He didn't remember even his name, let alone the name of the trees in front of an Italian woman's house.

Suddenly, he stood up and filled his glass with some water and looked at the mirror, over the toilet table, but the darkness didn't let him see the wrinkles of his face. Silence had haunted his soul. This silence also conquered all his furniture. The only thing that was standing against this silence was the sound of the refrigerator. He came out of the toilet, and took out another pill from the pack and gobbled it up, while staring at the window.

In the middle of all these silences, a voice was shaking him like an earthquake. This voice was with him everywhere, even inside the air plane. It was like a loud laughter or maybe painful cry. He considered himself a looser who had lost both his life and his bitter love. In fact, he was more like a dead, and the only thing, made him seems alive was his headache. He had packed to return to Iran. He was discharged from the hospital almost a week ago, because he suddenly got an intestinal problem. His friend Masoud said, if he had reached the hospital a little later, he would have died. His surgery lasted for three hours. Nobody knew what had happened to him. All the Iranian and Kurdish students tried to help him, but it was useless. Masoud said that all his hair turned white, during the past month.

He pulled aside the curtain again, laid on his bed and looked at his cell-phone.

Everyone was shocked by what happened to this funny, healthy guy …

He spent all his days by staring at the walls. He checked up on his phone repeatedly. "Whatever they say, I cannot live without you …"

"I stand against all of them."

He read this message and repeated it out loud. He was reading that message a hundred times a day, until he got tired and fell asleep.

In an hour, the plane would arrive in Tehran. His head was still hurting and that sound was striking again. He was trembling. Five months ago, he started studying for Doctorate at Milan University in Italy. He was supposed to go there first, and then he had a plan to take Awenya. Everything was going well, until one day Awenya sent him a message saying that, 'I am not ready, we cannot marry each other, please leave me alone.' At first, Hawre thought that it was only a joke, but when he called Awenya and noticed that his number had been blocked by Awenya, he got scared and called Awenya's best friend, Snoor. Same like Awenya, Snoor didn't answered him too.

He called them hundred times, but to no use.

That day was the beginning of his misery. He was only blaming himself for leaving Awenya, although he answered himself, "I had no other way. Something happened to her … her mother and Shawjwan…"

Suddenly, a voice woke him up!

A man who was sitting next to him on the plane, shook his shoulder and called him. After a while, Hawre answered him, "What, what happened?"

"Nothing, we have arrived.

The man approached him, "My son, you were hallucinating, I was afraid…"

Hawre who was drenched in a cold sweat, couldn't answer him and asked,

"Are you Kurdish too?"

"Yes, I am."

"Thirsty, I am thirsty."

The man called one of the flight attendants to bring him some water. Hawre took a pill out of his pocket and drank a sip of water. He remembered the letter he had written to Awenya a few days ago. *My love, you wrote to me it is over, but you don't know that, this end is end of all my hopes.*

"Sir, are you better now?"

Hawre looked at the man, but he couldn't talk, he only nodded his head, in agreement.

Awenya, my star, which dark night stole you from me?

"We are close, we will be there in half an hour."

He was sweating again; the air was dark and the plane was landing slowly. He felt that he lost his hope forever, and he failed everything: studying abroad, life with Awenya. *If I go out for studying, there were no excuses left for your mum and Shawjwan.*

He was weak and couldn't come down alone from the plane, that's why that man gave him a hand.

No one can take you away from me.

Hawre attached one of his romantic pictures with Awenya to the letter. He remembered that he posted the letter to Awenya's school.

15

It was a cold, cloudy afternoon on December. Rahman axa and Araaz were sitting inside the tent. Miss Zinat, Rozhan and Fariba, who hated Rahman axa and his family, wished for a flood to come and take Rahman axa's tent away. Miss Zinat, who heard a news about Rozhan's husband, Sabir, got curious and went to Rozhan's house quickly. Sabir's return was not important for Rozhan anymore. Rozhan said this to Fariba.

"Sabir's presence or absence are the same for me."

Rahman axa was making fire, while Araaz was sitting out of the tent.

"I'm coming, make the fire."

It was Keywan coming back from his job. He was carrying a big bag. Araaz went forward to help him. They brought the bag inside the tent.

"Where did you get all these drinks?"

Rahman axa snatched one of the bottles from Araaz's hand and put on his glasses while he reading the name of the bottle and spelled it, "Chi…chivaz."

"It is shiwaz, Rahman axa," Araaz spelled it.

"I know!" shouted Rahman axa, "I used to drink a lot of it."

Keywan brought a chair and sat next to fire and said, "I got very tired today."

"What kind of cargo did you have?"

"Everything: refrigerator, TV …mine was very heavy and the snow made it heavier. Kolbari is terrible, especially in this weather."

"Let's go inside. I am afraid people see us …"

"So, you didn't tell us where you got all of these!" Rahman axa asked again.

"We found it on our way back home. I thought it might be useful for this cold winter."

"Of course, it is useful."

Keywan drunk a glass of whisky and asked Rahman axa about the antique customer.

"I called him several times, but he didn't answer at all," Rahman axa answered.

Araaz, who drank a beer, put his hand on Keywan shoulder and said, "Don't worry, he will come soon."

"My wife is sick. I have to take her to Tehran."

Rahman axa got drunk gradually, his face turned red and from time to time he was singing. He stopped for a while and asked them:

"Tell me what is better than kissing a girl and touching her breasts? …too bad that I am not young enough for that …youth of this era are not like us, I don't know why?"

"The youth of this era haven't enough time to think about woman, kiss and breasts. They all live from hand to mouth."

Rahman axa had warmed up, he jumped from one branch to another, from girls to comrade Stalin and Smkoy Shkak[1].

---

[1] A kurdish chieftain and leaders in Rozhhalat.

Keywan was already tired, he got more tired with Rahman axa's words. Suddenly, voice of Shawjwan startled them, who called out her dad loudly."

"What happened, my daughter?"

"Come here please."

Rahman axa stood up and went with her. After them, Keywan left the tent without saying goodbye.

"That crazy girl says I'll kill myself," Shawjwan said to Rahman axa.

It has been two days since she went to school. She has locked herself inside her room and hasn't talked to anyone. After Rahman axa's family agreed with Hazhar's proposal, everything went well. They even bought rings for each other. Until one day a postman brought a letter to the school. It was written on it, For Awenya. At that very moment, Hazhar was in the dean's office. The principal of the school handed the letter to Hazhar and said, "It is for your fiancé." Hazhar looked at the letter and opened it. He got shocked when he saw the picture. That day, Hazhar went home early and didn't answer Awenya's call. He found the name of the person who sent the letter, on Faccbook and talked with Hawre until he found out about everything. Next day, in front of all the teachers, Hazhar crumpled the picture and letter and slammed it at Awenya's face, then he threw away the ring.

"You told me that you haven't been in any relationship before, traitor." He spat in her face and left the school forever. Awenya got shocked and bent down to pick up the picture. She didn't know what to do.

"I told you that you can't hide all these. You would have to tell Hazhar the truth."

How could you do this? said by Shawjwan, Hawre did everything only because of you and now he is coming back soon.

Unfortunately, Hawre also knew everything. You betrayed him, too.

Awenya's best friend, Snoor, didn't know how to help her.

She knew that escaping from this swamp seemed impossible.

"Awenya, my little girl, what happened?" Rahman axa knocked on the door.

"She has gone crazy," Shawjwan answered her dad. I just asked the same question, and she attacked me with a knife and now she wants to kill herself." Shawjwan answered, while she was laughing secretly and she mocked Awenya when she said, "it is result of betrayal."

After that day, Awenya didn't go to school. Most of the time, she stayed in her room, and didn't talk to anyone.

It had been several days since the internet was cut off. The phone network was also weak. People say that a big fight happened in the border villages, an Iranian military base had exploded and there were some victims. Some people believed that Guerrilla [1] did this, the other said that Peshmerge attacked. Rahman axa, who was fully drunk, believed that Komalla did this attack, he shouted, "They came again, the heroes of Mao and Stalin, the sons of Marx and Lenin, they come to destroy the palace of capitalism."

Araaz and Keywan was amazed that since the day, Keywan brought the drinks, Rahman axa had quit opium

---

[1] A Kurdish fighter and members of PKK is called Gurrilla

completely. After his lunch, Rahman axa would gather some woods, make fire then sit on a chair and drink whisky.

"What are you talking about, Rahman axa? What Komalla, Marx and Stalin. People said there were four Guerrillas in around Choman village who got besieged and one of them, who was an Illamian girl got martyred."

Keywan got scared by this news, and asked, "Are you sure they were Guerrilla? What about the martyr? Is she a girl or …?"

"I am not sure, I just heard it," answered Araaz.

Keywan who got shocked by the news stared at the fire and said,

"When will the war be over in the Middle East? When? When will this bloodshed end? Oh, we want freedom and peace." Rahman axa blamed USA for all the wars all over the world, but Araaz believed that Russia and China were responsible for the world misery. They always had argument about political issues.

"How dare you talk about Lenin, Stalin and Marx?" Rahman axa shouted.

"How dare! Is that so? God damn all of them. They were killers, only that bastard Stalin killed more than a hundred million people in Soviet Union."

"What did you say, you bourgeois!" Rahman axa couldn't control himself and stood up to attack Araaz.

16

"Oh, slow down, you hurt my lips again. Its scar hasn't gone yet. My lower lips are always swollen by your bite, Fariba."

"It is mine. I like it and I bite it."

"Will Rozhan stay at home tomorrow?" Araaz asked, while he hugged Fariba.

"No, she will go to her uncle's house."

"So, we have to take Dlir too."

"A little more, my horse." Fariba got horny.

Araaz was playing with her breasts and from time to time he asked,

"Do you like it?"

"Is Marlon sleeping?" Fariba asked.

"No."

"Does he like it again?"

"You know that Marlon always liked Ashmol."

Ashmol's barking changed their mood suddenly.

"Why is the dog barking, Araaz?"

"She got horny by your voice."

"Don't make jokes, she has been barking since the morning."

"Maybe she is afraid of Rahman axa," Araaz teased Fariba again.

"Do you love me, Araaz?"

"A little."

"Don't make me sad. I feel like you have changed."

Araaz put his hand in her hair and tickled her.

"Oh, don't do that. Dlir will wake up!"

"Didn't I tell you, not to say that again?"

"Ok, I won't say that again, but I feel that your kisses are not the same as our first day."

"Do you know, what I liked more on our first day?"

"No, you don't love me anymore!"

"I wanted to hug you, and hold you tight until I would melt in your arms. I like to be lost in your bright eyes."

"What would you do if I died?"

Araaz turned his back on her, in anger.

"Answer me, Araaz. If not, I'll bite you."

"I know that death is not so merciless."

"Tomorrow is Chlla[1] night, do you know that?"

Araaz turned to Fariba again,

"Tonight is also Chlla, let me see your mole."

"I want to bite your lips again."

"Impossible."

"Yes, possible."

"Please, it hurts a lot."

"For the last time."

"Ok, but don't bite it too hard!"

"I would like to have a house with wooden green windows!"

"Can you guess that Pomegranate seedlings we planted are grown now?"

---

[1] The first night of winter is called Yallda or Chlla

"Wooden window! Time of wooden window is over!"

"I say, Araaz, is there any wooden window left? Do people still make it?

I remembered my grandfather's house, his living room had two windows. The upper small hatch of one of the windows was always opened. There was a Vine tree in the yard, its branches had reached near the window. There were a Samovar and a pot, full of the pink Geranium."

"If Haji Baxtyar was alive, he would have made us wooden window," Araaz answered Fariba with a bitter laugh.

"There was also a big Mulberry tree in the yard, its fruits were red and tasty. At night, we used to look at the stars on the balcony. My aunt used to say, 'stars also fall in love, but their heart breaks and their deaths are the same."

"Don't make me laugh, Araaz."

"Look at the sky, I believe most of the stars are dead, they are only brightening in their dreams."

"You know that you haven't read a poem for me in a long time, Araaz!"

"It is because, you didn't write them."

"I wrote all of them. I was afraid that one day you look at me like a stranger, and leave me."

"What are you talking about?"

"Hurry up, read me a poem, Araaz!"

Like a snowflake in the evening of Yalda (chlla night)
I like to enter the heart of your little doll,
You looking at me
Me melting in your eyes
"You fooled me, with these words and won my heart.

"No, no, no, I dedicated my heart to you."

"People say that Yalda is the night of making love between Earth and Sky."

"We won't plant pomegranate this year. I like lemons and olives. I will make a crown out of olive leaves for you, like the queen of Rome and Greece."

"Lemon does not grow here."

17

"Mr Araaz, your car smells like gas."

"Rozhan is right, haven't you fixed it?" asked Fariba.

"I took it to the mechanic, but some broken parts are not available here, I have to bring it from Bokan."

Dlir was sleeping in Rozhan's arms. It was past eight in the morning, and the road was very slippery. There was a lot of snow. The cars were moving slowly in a line.

"The road is terrible; we shouldn't have come today. This fog has also reduced eyesight," Fariba said.

"It is not fog, but dust that no longer comes only in summer season. I promised to deliver these TVs today, the customer is waiting for us. Don't worry about the road, as soon as the sun rises, the fog will end."

They took Rozhan to her uncle's house, then they headed towards bazar to load the TVs.

People had gathered at the door of the café. One of the shopkeepers, named Rzgar Bag had a heart stroke. People say that he had lent a lot of goods to one Zanjani customer but the customer hadn't returned the money.

"Poor man."

"This is our bazar, if you do Kolbari, you will be hit with a bullet, or might be frozen in the mountain and become wolfs

150

food, or you may fall from a mountain and become crippled, or you will go bankrupt due to the rise and fall of Dollar prices, or they will gabble your money like this poor man and if you carry a cargo, sooner or later, you will have an accident on the road, not to mention the police's gunshot."

"You don't want anything, Fariba?"

"Look if he has any pills for headache."

The winter's power had defeated autumn; snow had come to conquer the earth. It snowed for an hour then stopped for a while and started to snow again, but the Sun couldn't show up for a bit. Dust became a permanent guest of the area. Seeing the blue sky became a dream."

"Where did you find it?" Fariba took the pill from him.

"The owner of café has a headache too. I also filled up the tea flask."

Araaz got into the car and they set off to Tabriz. In the car they talked about Rozhan.

"She is very sad," said Fariba.

Araaz remembered Rozhan's word, who was talking to Fariba inside the car.

"I have no luck, Fariba," cried Rozhan.

She said quietly and from time to time, wiped her tears with her hands.

"It was my mum's fault," continued Rozhan.

Like always, Fariba supported him, when she uttered secretly that she hasn't slept with him even for one time.

Fariba described this last part mutely, in case Araaz wouldn't notice it.

"I can't hear you, a little louder," Araaz said.

"For God's sake Fariba, let it be between us. I don't want even Mr. Araaz to know about this." Rozhan took a look at Araaz, who was cleaning the windows and continued.

"Sabir's parents knew about this issue from the beginning, but they didn't let me know. His parents took him to a Kurdish fortune-teller Sheikh for treatment. After the Sheikh prayed for him and gave him Zamzam[1] water, he told his parents that he will get better if he gets married. Miss Zinat explained all this to me. I knew about this problem from the beginning. I noticed that Sabir had more girlish feelings and I told him to see a doctor several times, but …

"After a couple of months, Sabir's breasts got bigger and bigger. So big that he was ashamed to go out." Rozhan told her that she gave him her bras.

"Didn't Rozhan mention, whether he has a penis or not?"

Fariba looked at Araaz with a smile and said,

"Off course their penis is not ordinary."

Rozhan said, "One day, Miss Zinat asked me about this topic in front of Hama and her mum. Hama who heard this started singing about it. He shouted, "Big breast and ball less, our groom Sabir dismissed."

"Not only Hama, but also our society in general, doesn't accept Sabir as a sick person. They all look at him like a doomed one."

"May God help, Miss Rozhan!"

"Can we visit the doctor today?"

"We have no more jobs, as we deliver the TVs, we will go directly to the doctor."

---

[1] A holy water in Islam, from the fountain in Mecca

The snow covered the forest. The road, forest and snow looked like a painting portrait in the rear view mirror.

"What did that man want from you, when he whispered in your ear?"

"Who? You mean Rahman axa?"

Fariba turned away her face in anger and said,

"Yes, Rahman."

"I wish, I knew what your problem is with this poor man and his family! He said that his wife likes cheese from Tabriz. He wanted me to bring him some cheese."

"Because they are pervert and rude, look at his younger daughter."

"This is not our problem, not even Rahman axa's problem."

"You don't know the reality; his elder daughter caused all those problems."

"Shawjwan? How?"

"As I see you know her name well …people say that poor boy left the school for ever. Some people play with others life. How could she do this to that poor guy. He did everything for her sake. He went to Europe to get that gypsy's approval, but that whore betrayed him as soon as she found a richer guy."

"People say that Hawre has returned. I asked Rahman axa, but he didn't know about that. Hawre sent Shawjwan a message that he will take his revenge."

"I don't know, but Rozhan told me he saw a thin guy who came to Rahman axa's door and started yelling and screaming." Rozhan said that the guy shouted loudly, 'How could you do this to me …You are a killer …You ruined my life'. I hope, no one would be like him."

"Separation due to death is much better than by betrayal …"

A heavy darkness ruled upon the snowy jungle. Dust and fog were mixed together. The road could hardly be seen. The cars were moving slowly on one line with their lights on. Under the lights of the cars, the road was showing itself for a while and then disappeared in the dust and fog.

"Fariba did you feed Ashmol?" asked Araaz.

"Yes, not to worry, the dog wanted to come with us, I didn't let her and hardly pushed her inside."

"I dreamt of my mother last night. In my dream, she was sitting on the door of our dilapidated house in Halabja. The Vane tree was in the middle of alley.

"'Hello, son, what happened? Are you coming to take the vane tree?'

"She had a cloche hat on her head that she decorated with a lot of amber stone.

"'Araaz, my son, didn't you find a green tobacco for me? I have almost run out of tobacco.'

"She was wearing a white blanket scarf and a green dress.

"'Mum, why didn't you wear a belt?'

"She laughed and said, 'I gave my belt to your father, he wanted to make a dress out of it for himself.'

"She put her hand in her pocket and took out a picture of my father. In the picture my dad was wearing that dress.

"'How do I look like, Halaw? Is it nice?'

"A classic tartan shirt that its colours were mostly green, red and white. For a moment the salad cups came to my mind.

"'You are very handsome man,' said mum, 'just like the first day you had come for me.'

"Some pictures were hanging on the tree.

"'Mum, it is Haji Baxtyar's picture!'

"'Be quiet, don't let your father notice that, he gets upset about that.'

"'For whom you roll the cigarette?'

"'I have guest, don't worry I will put less than the green tobacco.'

"Two people came out of nowhere and sat down without greeting. I feel that I knew them, or I know them but I can't remember. Their faces were not cleared. They took the cigarette from my mum, took a glance at it then they put the cigarette between their lips. My mum lit it for them. They looked at me and shook their heads. They inhaled the smoke for three times and suddenly two wings came out from behind their backs, but this time opposite to the angels of Baxtyar Ali[1]'s ship they turned into a fire and disappeared in the sky.

"'Hi, Miss Halaw, good morning."

"It was Homar Xawar, he had his kid on his arms. He was coughing huskily.

"'Hi, cousin Homar, what brought you here this morning?'

"'I want to take a look at the Kojilas, a demand for bitter gum is increased this year. Anything new about Kak Ahmad?'

"Without waiting for answer, he put his kid on my mum's arms and went towards the Kojilas and checked them.

"'Nothing. No gum, we got nothing this year.'

"I approached and looked at the Kojilas. Each one of them had got a pair of alive eyes inside. Homar Xawar collected the eyes, and put them inside his pocket sneakily."

"Araaz Araaz, watch out, that car coming towards us …"

---

[1] One of the contemporary Kurdish writers, especially novelist

Araaz was startled at her loud voice and suddenly pushed the brake pedal. A big truck came towards them. Araaz couldn't run away from that and the truck hit them severely and overturned Araaz's car. His car was completely crushed. Araaz pulled himself out through the window but whatever he tried; he couldn't open Fariba's door. Fariba's head and face was bloody. Araaz broke the window by a stone, but to no avail. Fariba got stuck and suddenly the car caught fire.

That night on the news, Rozhan saw a car that was overturned. At first, she wouldn't pay much attention, but when she saw one of Dlir's shoes, she noticed everything.

Police said that the truck hit them and the car got overturned, and then because of fuel leak, it exploded.

Rozhan, with tears in her eyes, called them several times, but their phone was off.

"In a car accident in Boukan Tabriz Road, unfortunately a mum and her child died and the husband also got severely injured." Most of the village heard of the accident. They were so sad about what happened to Araaz family! Rahman axa and Keywan searched around for Araaz but they didn't find any clues. Chief Salim also tried hard to find Araaz through the police office but he also came back empty-handed.

Days passed; January ended. In February, it snowed a lot. Miss Zinat got very excited about it. The roads were frozen, but Rahman axa had not packed his tent. Rozhan would see him some evenings along with Keywan making a fire. Ashmol was barking since sunset. After the accident, Rozhan took Ashmol up to her house, but Ashmol couldn't stay in one place and she barked a lot. She was missing Dlir and Fariba. One night, Ashmol got lost. Rozhan searched every place for her, but no use. At midnight, Rozhan was woken up by her barking. When Rozhan came down to her, she saw that Ashmol was standing on the stairs, shivering from the cold, and looking at Araaz's house and barking sadly.

For the first time, she saw a real tear. She realised that animals are more faithful than humans.

Rozhan hugged her and took her up, while she was crying.

Araaz's family visits was like a dream for Rozhan. They came unannounced and vanished quickly. Fariba, Dlir, Daya Halaw and Araaz were like a miracle for her loneliness.

"Oh, I miss Dlir so much. I wish, I never saw you." While Rozhan was smelling Dlir's clothes, she heard a strange sound downstairs. It was like a moaning and crying. She pulled aside the curtain and looked outside, but there was nothing there.

"Turn the TV down, Hama, I heard a sound."

"It is nothing, but sound of wolves," said Rozhan's mum.

"No, it is not, mum. It is a human moaning, just like someone is crying."

In the morning, Rozhan went down and knocked on the window of Araaz's house.

"Mr. Araaz, Mr. Araaz."

There were some footprints on the stairs.

It had been one month since the accident, and Rahman axa was sitting with Keywan inside the tent.

"Is there anything new, Rahman axa?" asked Keywan.

"Who are you? You asked me this a thousand times. I told you that the customer will call us soon and we have to be patient."

Keywan turned around, looked at Rahman axa and said,

"I am talking about Araaz."

"Oh, how should I know? You know that we searched every place for him."

157

It was evening and still snowing slowly.

"Would you like to drink some whisky?"

"Is there any for me?"

Keywan stood up and went inside the tent.

"Yes, we drank only half of it."

"Okay, pour me a little."

As usual, after two glasses of whisky, Rahman axa started to tell his stories; this time story of how he eloped with his wife Zara.

"I was a travelling salesman, who travelled all the villages around.

"The more I used to sell women's requirement, the women gathered around me …when I got tired, I used to go to visit an old woman, whose house was near the fountain. Most of the time, she was sitting in her door and knitting some cotton. One day, when I got there exhausted, she called on her daughter to bring me a glass of water. Her daughter, Zara, was so beautiful that I fell in love with her abruptly. I felt that she was some winged angel."

"Oh my God, not the winged angel, again."

"Trust me, their eyes and hair were the same. The old lady told me that she was engaged with Agha's[1] son, and she will marry in Nawroz, but it was obvious that Zara didn't like this arranged marriage. Then one day at the end of summer, I visited that village again. The old lady was not sitting in the door, but the door was opened. I knocked on the door and went inside the house. I saw Zara.

"'Hello, sir Rahman, my mum is not home, come in.'

---

[1] A title in old kudish society that regarded as high social class.

"That is all I wanted, so I didn't let her finish her words and entered immediately. A few hanged pictures, a mirror and a crack on the wall didn't reduce my fear for a bit. A cold sweat covered all my body. I looked at the kitchen. She was turning on the samovar, couldn't control myself anymore. I went to the kitchen for her and hugged her from behind.

"'Oh, don't do that, my mum is about to come back.'

"The same day, we ran to Bashur and stayed there for a few years."

The fire got weaker, Keywan wanted to ignite it that suddenly he shouted,

"Who are you? Rahman …Rahman axa." They were scared a lot and wanted to run, when a familiar voice said, "It's me Araaz."

"Araaz, is that you?"

Keywan ran towards him and hugged him tightly. His face was all wounds and scars. Rahman axa poured a glass of whisky for him. It was dark and Araaz had nothing to tell, he only shed a tear.

Ashmol's barking made Rozhan come down. Rozhan knocked on the Araaz's door again but no one answered.

"Let's go up, it is very cold outside, no one is there."

When Rozhan wanted to lift Ashmol up, suddenly one light of Araaz's room turned on, and the door opened. Ashmol ran inside quickly and when she saw Araaz, she sniffed him with all her power and started barking. Ashmol attached herself to Araaz's feet tightly.

"Mr. Araaz is that you?" shouted Rozhan, and she couldn't say anything more. She didn't believe her eyes. He was more like a confused soul than a human!!

"Hi, Miss Rozhan."

He shaved all of his hair. There was a big scar under his right eyes, and a burnt patch on his neck. Rozhan's eyes were full of tears, but she didn't say anything. Ever since that night, she was preparing food for Araaz, and Araaz was washing the dishes and he returned the dishes back and put them on Rozhan's stairs. It was snowing constantly for some days. The weather forecast said that It would snow for a week. Miss Zinat was happy about that, but she also uttered that after a heavy snow, something bad will happen. Early in the morning of the next day, Rahman axa and Keywan came to take Araaz for hunting. At first, Araaz didn't agree to join them, but after Keywan insisted, he agreed and they took Ashmol with them too.

Rahman axa prepared his hunting gun.

"This gun is not an ordinary one, my cousin sent me this gun from Hawlir[1]. The gun is American."

In the evening, they returned. Araaz, who was very tired, went inside quickly with a rabbit in his hand. He sat on the stairs and lit up a cigarette and called Rozhan.

"If you like rabbit meat, I brought one."

Rozhan came down quickly and took the rabbit. It was strange for her that during this time returning home, Araaz refused to look straight into her eyes and he turned his face away while she was talking to him.

"Mr. Araaz, you seem better now."

Araaz inhaled deeply on his cigarette and looked at the sky,

"Thanks, I am better now."

---

[1] The capital city of Kurdistan regional government. It also in Arabic language called Erbil.

It was snowing non-stop, as Miss Zinat said, "It snowed up to the waist. There was no one outside." There were only some footprints of a fox, who may have come out because of hunger. A heavy silence conquered the village until the scream of Rahman axa's wife, Zara, broke the silence.

"Help me."

Araaz arrived first. As usual, Rahman axa was sitting on his chair. He had worn a green blouse. A dagger was stuck on his chest. A hand-made dagger! Just like the dagger that I saw on my first day on the wall at the yard, like the dagger that was tattooed on Rahman axa's arm. The blood trace was continued to the river. Keywan arrived there nervously.

After a couple of days, his wife Zara told the police that a Persian man had visited him the other day.

Rahman axa was buried in the old cemetery behind his house. The grave digger dug his grave with great difficulties. Imam prayed for him quickly, while he was shivering, and he left soon. Only his wife and his daughter Shawjwan, were ready for his ceremony. None of them cried for him, and thus the legend of Rahman axa Ashpoka ended.

18

It was snowing and he didn't remember when it started, but he remembered his last night's dream that in the middle of summer, he was lying under the shadow of half-burned willow tree by the river, when suddenly a dark cloud covered the sky. It started snowing and it went on. The screams of his wife woke him up.

"Mouse, mouse, wake up! There is a mouse in the house." He took the blanket off him and looked at his wife. His wife was holding her head in her hands, she also had dreamt of a mouse like previous nights.

"No, it wasn't a dream, I saw a mouse in the clothes," said Keywan's wife. Keywan got up, turned on the light and brought a glass of water for her.

"It is nothing, drink it." She drank the water and pointed to the heater. It had cooled down; it ran out of oil. He took the oil tank and filled it up from the barrel in the yard.

"Outside is cold. It is still snowing." He turned the heater and warmed himself in front of it for a couple of minutes.

"Why are you looking at me like that?"

"Nothing." She hid under the blanket, but her eyes were on Keywan.

"Is he coming with you?"

"I don't know," Keywan answered and looked out from the window, and he went to the kitchen and brought a bowl of yoghurt and a piece old bread to eat.

"Do you want me to make tea for you?" she asked.

"No," Keywan answered, "you just try to sleep."

"I can't sleep, I am afraid of sleep, because I wake up by bad dreams. By the way, did you find your hat?"

"No," Araaz said, "I saw it in Rahman axa's tent."

"So, you mean it is gone?"

Keywan took out a black plastic bag from the fridge, and he lifted his boots from the shelf and put his hands inside one of them to see if the glue stuck well.

"Let's check it, when it gets wet, but the glue was the best type." Keywan put on his pants. "Where are my socks?"

"Look around the heater, if not there, we have many socks in one bag in the other room."

"All are mismatched."

"You haven't been invited for the wedding, what difference does it make?" He put on different coloured socks and put on his jacket. "Should I turn the lights off?"

"No. no, turn on the TV, too." The front door was blocked by snow. He put on his jacket and put the black bag on his head. The road hasn't been taken yet; the land was in a heavy sleep. He stopped for a while, and looked at his phone. Araaz was also coming out, he put his hands in his pocket. He had a bag on his head same like Keywan, but Araaz's was blue. They were not in the mood for small talks, so they only nodded their head to each other and started walking. It has been a couple of days since Araaz went to Kolbari with Keywan. It was Rahman axa's suggestion. The alleys got shocked to see these two poor men. They smelled like death. Araaz and Keywan had the same feeling for the alleys, everything was strange for them. After this all, they were also afraid of alleys and streets. It was like death was lying in wait for them. Night, snow, darkness and alienation of two hopeless men, who both had a bag on their head, created a frightening scene. Some blood and crow's feather had been spilled in front of Chief Salim's shop. The mosque has not been opened yet, for Morning Prayers, but the sound of an old man, who was spitting loudly could be heard. It had been a few days since the borders were closed again, nobody knew the reason, some said that some fights had happened there and the others believed that they have a plan to close it permanently. They were all rumours. Kolbari was very difficult in the snowy weather. A few days ago, two brothers were trapped under the avalanche. The corpse of the elder brother named Farhad was found, but the younger one was still under the snow. Keywan went in front and cleared the way and Araaz was fallowing him. Araaz was thinking about Keywan.

"His hopeless face, his lost son, his sick wife and his unclear future. He is worse than me." Keywan knew that his wife won't live for long. She had liver disease. He needs big money to save her, and by Kolbari they couldn't make such a big amount. His mum, Miss Zinat said that her bride was the most beautiful woman in the village, but the grief of her lost son broke her down and made her sick.

The driver checked the tire's air by kicking it. When he saw them, he got shocked and shouted at them, "God damn you, what is that on your head, you scared us." Although the night released the sky, but the darkness still prevailed and the white colour of snow was the only hope to brighten up the land. The bus was waiting for Keywan and Araaz on the other side of Shirwan spring. They got into the bus and greeted everyone quietly. Only a young guy, who was sitting in the front seat answered them. They looked for empty seats.

"Those two in the middle are empty." The driver pointed to the seats and looked at them through the mirror. He was coughing and prayed before he started the engine, and then he turned on the bus, but it wouldn't start, he tried again, but the engine wouldn't start. He tried several times but it was no use.

"It's not working, you have to get off and push the car." Most of the passengers got off to push the car. Keywan took a look at Araaz who was sitting near the window, "You stay I will go."

After many efforts, the car started and they set off. It was so cold inside the bus.

"Please turn on the heater, we are about to freeze."

"Let the engine warm up a little, you big baby, you are not trapped in Qandil Mountains." The driver answered them with a soft voice, while looking at them through the mirror. They were all grumbling in their seat.

"We never saw your car work well for once."

"You can warm up the car a little earlier." The road was slippery, that's why the driver was moving slowly. Everyone was quiet and some were sleeping. Araaz was looking outside. The road divided the cemeteries into two parts, that's why here at the graveyard the dead never feel alone.

Araaz was thinking about his family in the bus; Fariba and Dlir burnt in front of his eyes and he couldn't do anything to save them. The only thing left of Fariba was her necklace. Her last look inside the ruthless fire was penetrating inside the depth of Araaz's soul.

The driver glanced at the flask, and he gave the glass to his assistant.

"Pour me a glass of tea." He put the glass on the dashboard to cool it down, then he lit a cigarette and looked at the passengers through the mirror. His mirror was broken in half, a rosary was hung on it, and in the top part of the mirror there was a goat horn for protection against evil eye. *"Superstition" I wish, I knew who has evil eye upon this old junk.*

The passengers were waking up slowly, the blubbering started, but Keywan and Araaz were silent. Keywan took of the bag from his head and folded it up. In the front row seats, two passengers were smoking. Smoke, gas scent was mixed with the smell of sweat and made it hard to breathe. In the bus, everyone was talking about different topics. One of that two, who were smoking, narrated that last week his leg got dislocated and he got trapped in house for a week.

"What did you do? How did you recover?"

He turned around and glanced at Keywan and said,

"God bless, Miss Zinat who treated me well, believe me, it hurt me to death. After treatment, she wrapped my leg with a domestic egg. It still hurts, but I feel much better now."

"God bless her. What could we do without Miss Zinat? Last year I got awful disease, I couldn't move. I couldn't even perform my prayers. Even though I visited several doctors, it was useless, until one day, my mum brought Miss Zinat home. As soon as she saw me, she said, 'Your bellybutton is displaced'. She treated me for two sessions. I haven't experienced that pain since last year."

Keywan smirked when he heard those words, and he talked to himself, "This belly-button, …ha ha! My mum treated my poor wife more than a hundred times, but it had no use."

It was about to be dawn, but the sun was hiding itself behind the clouds. Araaz heard the conversation of two passengers behind, who were talking about the Referendum of Bashur with enthusiasm.

"God! May be with us to get free finally, and they will declare Kurdish government quickly."

"I am not so positive about that. Turkey and Iran already closed their borders. They threatened us."

"Turkey and Iran are not important, America is …"

Suddenly, the driver stopped the vehicle to pick up a passenger on the way. The driver drank all his tea, then he wiped his moustache and through the mirror signalled the new passenger to sit on an extra chair in the middle of the bus. After that, he took out his next cigarette, lit it up and drove away. Araaz felt that he knew this man.

"I saw him somewhere, oh the beets seller …"

But the beets seller didn't recognise Araaz.

"Hello, bro, you don't recognise me?"

"Hello, bro, no I am sorry."

"Do you remember the other day; I found my own book among your books."

"Yes, oh, yes what was your name? Awat, Aso, …"

"Araaz."

"Yes, Mr. Araaz what are you doing here?"

"I was about to ask you the same question."

The beets seller took a look at the first row, and got closer to Araaz.

167

"Please close that window, it is very cold, the wind comes inside."

The beets seller turned around and looked at him.

"I tried hard; it can't be closed completely."

"What should I tell you. Mr. Araaz! Life is not going well, we gave birth to another child, selling beets was not enough, and beside that job, I do Kolbari from time to time."

Keywan, who was sitting between them, took a deep breath and crumbled his bag and said, "God never forget us."

The beets seller looked at Keywan with a bitter smile, "God, you mean that old story, that human made it due to their weakness and loneliness, and then bowed to him."

"Human of this era are lost."

"Humans won't feel alive, unless they rebel."

"Baxtyar Ali says when human rebel, they become happy creature.

"No happiness equal to happiness of rebellion."

Araaz took the bag from Keywan, folded it and said,

"What kind of rebellion?"

"Human's rebel against himself or forcing him to rebel?"

"Baxtyar Ali doesn't say which rebellion is happiness. In my opinion, when a person rebels against himself, he would try to destroy whatever is in his mind. A great war against the imposed ordinary beliefs begins. The first step of this rebellion is inner uprising. Permanent and endless war. Freedom is the result of this rebellion, the thing that Baxtyar Ali called happiness."

"What about making the people rebel?"

"Until a person is not destroyed mentally, he won't rebel, he won't up rise until his soul get wounded. When his soul get wounded, when his hope and dreams before their birth, die in his heart, he would be destroyed and a terrible silence covers his life. The silence, that gives way to death and destruction. After that, the uprising of such a person is the destruction of his surroundings. Rebellion against the world turns to a fire, that burns and eventually he becomes a fearful creature, not a happy human."

Keywan took his bag from Araaz and looked at the torn hat of beet seller and said, "We are neither happy nor scary, we are dead and powerless. We could not rebel at all, neither against ourselves, nor against the world."

"Have your tickets ready!"

The driver assistant was a young man, he was in his twenties, his voice was horrible. He wore a green jacket. He collected the money and put it in his pocket. Keywan paid for all three, although the beet seller was not accepting first.

"We arrived; may God be with you."

They headed towards Kak Ahmad's teashop on the base of Sorkiw Mountain. The beet seller called Kak Ahmad from a far, "HI, Kak Ahmad, do you want any company?"

A young man who was standing in the door answered him, "What are you doing here?"

Keywan, Araaz and beet seller entered and sat around a table.

"Where is Kak Ahmad?"

"Jalal? Jalal, bring them tea Kak Ahmad went to Sullymani yesterday, he will come back soon. Do you want food?" Araaz and Keywan didn't eat, but the beet seller ordered an Omelette.

"Please bring me onion and pepper too."

"Okay." Kak Ahmad's teashop was on the base of Sorkiw Mountain. That part located on the border. It didn't belong to either Iraq or Iran. First it was a small teashop, more like a shelter, but later the job went well and Kak Ahmad added a kitchen and a bedroom to it.

The beet seller said that nobody knows about Kak Ahmad's past, nobody knows where he is from! They say he is Krmanj[1] and he could speak Kalhori[2] well. It was the first time for Araaz to visit this place. He stood up and looked outside, with a glass of tea in his hand. A wonderful scene of Choman River was circling among the snowy jungle.

"Do you still have your books?" asked Jalal.

The beet seller, who swallowed a big piece of onion, answered him with a full mouth after his last bite,

"Haven't you stopped reading yet?"

"For God's sake, swallow your food first, then answer me!"

"Only novels remain."

"Next time you come here, bring me Kazantzakis novel!"

"Which one?"

"*Freedom or Death.*"

He drank some coke after it.

"Haven't they found Azad's corpse yet?" beet seller asked.

"Not yet, many people came to find him."

"He might be alive, why you say corpse?"

"In this cold weather, it seems impossible, he was trapped under a huge snow pile."

"May God have mercy on their parents, they didn't even bury Farhad. They are waiting to find Azad."

---

[1] The kurd of northern Kurdistan

[2] Kurdish accent, saidn more in Rozhhalat

Farhad and Azad were two brothers, both under 20. They were Kolbar. An avalanche fell off and trapped them. The same day, the elder brother, Farhad, was found dead, but they still searching for Azad's trace.

They came out of the teashop and saw an old man who wore Faranji[1]. His hair and bread were matched with the snow. Keywan said that every day, this old man is seen in a different village. Sometimes he came by to visit Kak Ahmad.

"Good morning, boys, be careful. There were heavy gunshot last night. Keywan, like always, got scared, when he heard that a fight happened somewhere."

"I heard that it was mine explosion." It was Jalal who was shouting from the window.

"Is anybody injured?"

"I don't know, but people said, they saw a bloody footprint down, near the old army base."

Keywan got scared and his face turned pale. The snow stopped but a dark cloud covered the mountain. Keywan climbed the mountain like a crazy one, and they followed him: Araaz and the beet seller.

The old man screamed, "Don't go there, it is full of mines over there." But nobody heard him.

Everybody knew that Keywan's son is Guerrilla. They all knew that how much Keywan had suffered after the Islamic Revolution of Iran. He and his sick wife only had one son! It was a difficult uphill, but not for a people who climbing the harder cliffs with a heavy load on their back, were their daily works.

---

[1] A kind of old woolen clothes for the cold weather

They found a bloody footprint and chased it; the wind stokes them hardly in their faces.

"Come here, come here," screamed Keywan.

They got to Keywan quickly. It was an amputated leg. A little lower, under an oak tree, he found the lifeless body of his son, his only son.

The snowy mountain turned to blood colour and the sky became dark. He stood in front of his son, who leaned back against the oak tree, with a calm face and his gun was still in his hand. He seemed not to be a dead, more like he was sleeping in a cold death. Keywan rubbed his frozen face and hugged him tightly and he took his amputated leg. The beet seller cremated the body. Tears were frozen in Keywan's eyes. The wounds of his soul were reopening again.

Gunfire started.

Araaz shouted, "Don't shoot us, our cargo is a lifeless body!" A bullet hit the beet seller's head and he fell on the ground.

On the road, the old man was crouching, next to some corpses …